Naughty Elf: Twinkle
TL Travis

Sapphire Publishing

This book is a work of fiction. Names, characters, places, and incidents either are products of the author's imagination or are used fictitiously. Any resemblance to actual events or locales or persons, living or dead, is entirely coincidental.

Copyright 2024 by TL Travis

All rights reserved, including the right of reproduction in whole or in part in any form.

Published by Sapphire Publishing

Formatting by TL Travis

First Issue 2024

This book is licensed to the original purchaser only. Duplication or distribution via any means is illegal and a violation of International Copyright Law, subject to criminal prosecution and upon conviction, fines and/or imprisonment. This eBook cannot be legally loaned or given to others. No part of this eBook can be shared or reproduced without the express permission of the publisher.

NAUGHTY ELF: TWINKLE

NO AI/NO BOT. We do not consent to any Artificial Intelligence (AI), generative AI, large language model, machine learning, chatbot, or other automated analysis, generative process, or replication program to reproduce, mimic, remix, summarize, or otherwise replicate any part of this creative work, via any means: print, graphic, sculpture, multimedia, audio, or other medium. We support the right of humans to control their artistic works.

Contents

1. Chapter One — 1
2. Chapter Two — 6
3. Chapter Three — 20
4. Chapter Four — 36
5. Chapter Five — 49
6. Chapter Six — 65
7. Chapter Seven — 87
8. Chapter Eight — 102
9. Chapter Nine — 116
10. Chapter Ten — 132
11. Chapter Eleven — 147
12. Chapter Twelve — 159
13. Chapter Thirteen — 170

About TL Travis — 182

Other books by TL Travis — 183

Chapter One

TWINKLE

"Twinkle!"

Santa Twenty-Seven's growly voice rumbled down the corridor. Every machine stopped and the heads attached to the elves running them turned my way. Nosey little bees.

I shrugged and stood, took my time straightening my clothes and applied more lip gloss before making the twenty-foot walk of shame, though none of that showed on my face. I was the epitome of calm, cool, and collected though

I was anything but on the inside. I was Twinkle, for the love of Christmas. The best dressed, most well put together, near perfect, except for that one pesky mole on my back that I got removed. Scratch that, perfect elf.

With a penchant for mischief.

Just a smidge.

"Yes, Santa twenty-seven." My nonchalant attitude only exacerbated his anger.

Steam came from his ears, and his skin was an ugly shade of red, slightly darker than his Santa suit. His face contorted as he growled my name.

"Twinkle."

"Oh, you know how I love it when you get all growly with me." I winked and swayed my hips as I approached his desk, knowing full well I'd pushed him too far.

'You've been warned time and again not to mess with the naughty and nice lists. Those aren't your concern, they belong to..."

I cut off his tirade. Another thing about me he despised. No wonder year after year my stocking was filled with coal.

"Merlin." I blew on my nails, they still hadn't completely dried. "Perfect Merlin handles the perfect list." Wasn't my fault the fool left his computer unattended. The list beckoned me from across the room. Who was I to ignore such a grand gesture?

Santa rose and banged his fists on the desk, and I jumped. "Enough!"

I'd never seen him this angry in all the decades I'd worked for him in Santa's Village. The elves who never made it this far were jealous of those of us who landed jobs here. We were considered the elite having worked this close to the many Santas at the North Pole. Yes, I said many. How did you think they hit all those stops around the world in a single night?

"It's going to take a team of elves and a lot of overtime to fix what you've done."

One little delete button, and you'd have thought I fed his beloved reindeer laxatives.

Again.

Yeah, shoveling reindeer poo while following Blitzen nineteen, yes multiple Santas equal multiple generations of reindeer, around for three days straight was punishment enough. Lesson learned and all that. Or so one would've thought.

Hey, I never claimed to be the brightest elf in the village. Just the best dressed and most handsome one.

It was like I just couldn't help myself. Mischief should've been my name, yet I somehow ended up with Twinkle. Though I do shine like the beacon of light that I'm named for.

"You've changed out salt for sugar and ruined cookies. You've fed my favorite reindeer laxatives. Poor fellow was afraid to eat for a week. But this," he tapped a chubby finger to the pile of papers on his desk. "This was the last straw!" Santa only had one volume when addressing me—loud. And angry. So very angry.

Year after year I watched the same kids on the good list get presents while the bad ones received coal. How was it that the Santas got to decide who was truly bad? Didn't seem fair to me. I mean, I'd have taken a pair of scissors to my sister's hair too if it looked like a rat's nest. Little Jimmy in Des Moines had the right idea. Now her hair would grow back nice and shiny and stay that way. As long as she washed and brushed it, that was. See, problem solved and oh so helpfully.

I shivered at the thought. My hair was perfectly coiffed under this ridiculous hat we had to wear as part of our uniform, for which I hated. Every red and white piece of material. Don't get me started on the green, that shade did nothing to highlight my attributes, and the pointy shoes. Ugh. Horrible choice.

I did get written up for that present swap though, but I refused to back down and said my piece. Please, like I didn't know hair and make-up. Mine was flawless, after all, as was I.

"No. More. Twinkle."

Shoot, I'd forgotten about him. Were we still at this?

"Understood, Santa twenty-seven."

"No. I'm serious. You are officially relieved of your duties as inventory elf effective immediately."

"But..."

Sweet boughs of holly. What had I done?

Chapter Two
Monty

Knock-knock.

Who in their right mind had balls big enough to knock on my door on Christmas, no less, in the middle of a snowstorm, and during hibernation. Likely one of my siblings looking for a fight. I whipped the door open, prepared to throw down with whoever was there but there was no one in sight. No foot or paw prints in the snow and a quick sniff of the air confirmed no one was near.

"Huh, what gives?" My eyes landed on a box nearly buried in the snow. I looked forward to this storm. It meant none of my nosey family would be out and about bothering me. Or so I thought. Sadly, some of us required less sleep during these long winter months than the others. I was not one of them. *Get a mate*, they said. *You're such a hermit. Bears aren't meant to hibernate year-round.*

Oh yeah, watch me.

I'd purposely built my log cabin on the outskirts of our land far away from their prying eyes and constant meddling. So what if I was in my thirties and not mated? Who needed someone to tell them what they should or shouldn't do. Pick this up, clean up that mess.

Fuck. That. Shit.

I was an alpha and that meant I was in charge.

I slid the box free and knocked the snow off and took a sniff. You never knew what one of the clans was up to and it was better to be safe than sorry. I gave it a quick shake and something heavy rattled around, so I took it inside and sat it on the coffee table and went to make a cup of hot tea with honey.

Yes, I said it. A bear shifter and his honey. Go ahead, make all the jokes you want but honey *is* a staple in my house.

While I waited for the tea to steep, I opened the gift. "Huh, wonder where this ugly carving came from?" No note in the box, no artist signature on the statue. What the hell? I grabbed my tea, figured I could deal with this after a long nap when a "POP" rang through the air.

Out of the statue came a strange little man with pointy ears. He first straightened his clothes and then his hair, and twirled, like straight up did a perfect pirouette spin until he saw me and froze.

"What're you looking at you big hairy ape?"

The urge to hang him upside down by his pointy toes was strong. I snarled, baring my canines in warning. "Who are you and how did you find me?"

"I've never seen you at the North Pole before. Are you new? What does Santa have you doing? Are you my new babysitter?"

"Look, I don't know who you are..."

"Twinkle."

"Or how you got here," I continued, barely controlling the urge bite him. "But you need to leave. Now!" I growled and he jumped a foot in the air. A warped sense of satisfaction rippled through me.

"*Avec, pleasure.*" He flipped his hair as though it were long enough to do so, sashayed over to the door and flung it open, then stared out into the snowstorm. "This isn't the North Pole."

"No, it's my home and my land and you're trespassing."

He stomped his tiny foot and groused. "Fizzle sticks. Santa twenty-seven, what have you done?"

"Shut the door, you're letting the snow in."

"Humph," he huffed and slammed it shut. "Grr, Santa twenty-seven." He continued to curse under his breath as he paced the floor, many of his words related to sugary confections and what I'm guessing was a mall Santa that pissed him off.

No clue who this Santa fella was but that little growl of his was quite entertaining. "What kind of shifter are you?" I tugged on his ears.

"Ouch!"

"Sorry, never saw a shifter with pointy ears is all."

"I'm an elf, not a shifter. What's wrong with you?" Twinkle huffed again and rubbed his ears. "Banished. I can't believe Santa did this to me."

"Banished? Oh, no, no, hell to the mother fucking no." There was no way in the western hemisphere this strange little man was staying here. "You need to find a hotel." Was a waste of words to mention that. The nearest town would take a couple hours to get to in this blinding storm and there was no way in hell I was taking him anywhere.

He stared blankly up at me and blinked a few times. "You said a very bad word. I bet you're on the naughty list. What's your name?" Hands on his hips like he was suddenly the one in charge.

"Um, Monty?"

Huh, maybe he was.

"That sounded like a question, do you not know your own name?"

The amount of attitude this tiny package held was impressive, but it was time to take him down a few pegs. "Look, Omega, I don't know who you are or how the hell you got here but it's obvious, based upon the storm outside, you're stuck for a while." Couldn't fight back the yawn that came, it was well past naptime for me. "I'm going to bed."

Twinkle huffed. "Fine."

"Fine." Was mimicking childish? Of course it was, but being irritated and tired, it was all I had.

I woke to the smell of food. Took me a minute to remember I wasn't alone.

"Smells good," I grumbled, in dire need of coffee. As I started the pot and swung around I realized the place had been... "Did you b-dazzle my home?" What the holy hell. There were Christmas lights everywhere.

"Yes," Twinkle danced through the room to of all things, yule tide carols.

"Where did all of this come from?"

Fuck. Me.

"Oh, Kody came by. Then he brought his wife Grizelda back with him. Then your mom, Sandy, she is so sweet, was here. She brought the stew you smell on the stove. I had a wonderful time meeting your family." Twinkle didn't stop dancing the entire time he spoke.

"How long have I been asleep?" And how much sugar had he consumed to have created this infernal holiday scene.

"Three days. I was so bored. Then Kody came by to check on you and I told him about the North Pole and how I made Santa twenty-seven mad and got banished here. Then he came back with everyone else, and they brought me the lights," Twinkle clapped and hopped up and down, admiring their obnoxious handywork. "Isn't it amazing?"

"It's something all right." Wait. "Did you say everyone else?"

"Yes. I can't believe you slept through all the noise. We sang carols and baked cookies and played games with the kids."

Fuck, I'd never hear the end of this.

"Wait, how did they get here? Isn't it snowing?" I ran to the window and as expected, stared out at the blinding white scenery.

"Snowmobiles!" He continued to dance and sing like I wasn't there.

Great. "Are you dusting?"

"Yes, your place was a mess."

Nothing phased this guy.

"You moved my furniture?"

"Your brothers helped me. This works better when everyone is here. Plenty of room instead of bunched up like you had it. Better flow."

This miniature menace had made a bigger mess than he knew. Even with the cleaning.

"That's because I don't want everyone here. Ever." What part of leave me alone did these people not understand?

"Don't be such a grouch. Your family is so nice, and they love you." Twinkle stuck his tongue out and completed a perfect dismount off the chair he'd stood on.

"How much sugar have you had?"

"Not enough. It's time to eat. Sit." Twinkle danced over to the kitchen and proceeded to pull bowls from the cupboards to dish up the stew. "Why aren't you sitting?"

"You're not the boss of me." *Real mature, Monty.* What was it about this yahoo that reduced me to a level of immaturity I hadn't had since my primary years? Reluctantly, I sat, I mean, I was hungry after all. Three days with no food makes Monty a grouchy bear. Who was I kidding? I was terminally grouchy.

"There you go." With a swish in his step and a face filled with pride, he sat our bowls down and took a seat across from me. "Ooh, I almost forgot the bread."

I'm not sure this guy even knew how to walk like a normal person. His movements were a combination of skips, dances, and the occasional bunny hop. Hey, if they got through on snowmobiles maybe they could take Twinkle into town to find a room and possibly a bus ride out of Kodiak.

"Did anyone take you into town yet?" Perfect way to broach the subject without being my usual dick self.

Twinkle stopped bouncing and turned those big blue eyes on me. "No. Do they need to?"

Well fuck. Maybe I couldn't do this. Or maybe, I just needed more sleep.

"They're coming over later. I can ask if you have a list written out for me to go off of. Maybe they can take me to run your errands?" Far too joyful and willing to help was Twinkle. From what I'd gathered he had a penchant for mischief, and I had no clue if I could trust him.

"Who is coming over?"

"Your family, silly." He rolled his eyes and slurped his soup from the spoon. "This is really, really, really..."

I had to stop him before another song burst forth. "I got it, you like the stew."

"You're grouchy. No wonder you live alone." Twinkle groused as he crossed his arms over his chest. His bottom lip jutted out.

Now he was getting it. "Yes that's exactly why." *knock, knock*. "Ugh, I chose to live so far away from home to avoid this."

"Yay!" Twinkle clapped and cheered as he skipped to the door. "They're here!"

"Why aren't you hibernating?" I groaned as every. Last. Member. Of my family came inside.

"We don't require the sleep you do, dear brother." Kody winked and patted my shoulder like there was a known secret between us. Trust me, there was not.

"More like hiding from the world," Dad added. "We're shifters. Yes, we take long naps during the winter months but none of us sleep through the entire season. Save for you, Monty, and I still believe you're hiding and not hibernating."

Fucking astute man got on my last nerve.

Momma shooed him away before it turned into a wild wrestling match as it did most times the males in the LeClaire Clan gathered.

"We met your Twinkle." The pleased tone in Momma's voice did nothing to assuage my foul mood.

"He's not my anything, Momma. He pissed someone off and landed himself here. I'm sure it was a miscalculation, and he was meant to be delivered elsewhere." Like Antarctica, but I chose to leave that snide comment out.

"Hush, you. He might be a little eccentric." Momma patted my arm. "But he'll do."

"He'll do what?"

She gave me that look.

"Oh hell no." I couldn't back away fast enough until I hit the back of the couch and flipped over it. "Fuck!"

Silence rang out and every set of eyes was on me, including Twinkle's.

"Monty, watch your language," Momma scolded. "Kody, help your brother up."

"Monty," Kody held his hand out and I brushed it off. "You know as well as I do there is no way on this snow-covered mountain that tiny thing found his way here on his own. He was sent here for a reason. The way he got here may be...unique."

"He was a statue. In a box. On my porch. In the middle of a snowstorm that was delivered on Christmas day."

"Exactly."

And mother rejoined the conversation. From the sounds of it, one of many the family had already had while I slept.

Remind me again, why I woke?

Oh yeah, food.

Fucking bear senses.

"No, Momma. It's a firm No. No. No. No. Did I say no already?" I may have stomped my foot which did nothing to help plead my case. She gave me that knowing glare all mother's perfected during childbirth. "No."

"What the hell was that?"

Twinkle squealed and ran straight to the pile of boxes that appeared, much like he had, out of thin air. "Santa sent my stuff!"

Atop the boxes sat a red envelope. Twinkle opened it and silently read it. When he was done his face matched the envelope, and his hands shook.

"Twinkle? What's wrong?" When he didn't respond, I slid the letter from his fingers.

Twinkle,

In case you haven't guessed by now, your antics and bad behavior have forced me to banish you from the North Pole for which you may never return. As part of that punishment, you've been sent to your mate.

If you do not complete the mate bonding prior to this coming Christmas you will return to the statue state in which you were delivered for all eternity.

Santa twenty-seven

"Fuck!"

"Uncle Monty said a bad word," Kalib, Kody and Grizelda's oldest, tattled.

Before I could stop her, Momma squealed and riled the family up. Twinkle snuck off down the hall and I followed him.

"Twinkle?" I knocked on the door to the spare room. Guess he'd already claimed it as his. "Are you okay?" I jiggled the knob and since the door wasn't locked, I slowly entered. Wasn't sure if he was a shoe throwing elf or what I'd walk into, but clearly the story he told about Santa was true. The site I found nearly broke my heart.

If I had one it would've, that was.

Twinkle was curled up in the fetal position in the middle of the bed. Tears streamed down his face as he clutched onto my childhood bear. "Hey, how'd you get that?" I thought my Momma Had long since discarded.

Back on track, Monty.

"How could he do that? All those years I worked for him."

Somehow he managed to put the words together between the sobs.

"Well, imagine my surprise to not only find out Santa was real, but to have an elf who was delivered to me as was supposed to be my...my mate?"

My brothers and sisters all found their mates in the bear community and on their own. Who did I end up with? A pointy eared, over sugared, snarky ass elf. An elf. A real live, fucking elf. Who knew they really existed? Twinkle was easier to deal with when I just thought he was insane, and now I had no clue what to do.

"Look." He sat up and tossed the bear aside. "I don't want to be here anymore than you want me to be but I'm doing my best to make the *best* of it. If I don't—" His bottom lip quivered, and I felt the urge to take him in my arms and nearly acted up on it. *Nearly*.

I sat on the edge of the bed, not too close. The moment was already uncomfortable enough. "Let's just take this one day at a time, all right?"

Twinkle sighed. "Okay."

Chapter Three

TWINKLE

"Boys," Monty's mom, Sandy began as she stepped inside the room. When she saw me, whatever she was about to say was forgotten. "Monty, why don't you go play with the little ones for a few minutes."

As soon as the door shut behind Monty, she sat beside me. "Twinkle, first of all, I owe you an apology."

Wow, wasn't what I expected her to say at all. "You do?"

"Yes. It's sad to admit but as children the idea of Santa being real is everything to us. Then when we catch our parent's placing presents under the tree that childhood dream vanishes. So when you told us you came from the North Pole and Santa fired you, well," she patted my knee. "Let's just say my belief in your words wasn't strong and for that I must apologize."

"I'm so sorry you lost your beliefs. The Santas work hard to keep the dream alive in the children in the hopes they'll carry it with them forever. Those beliefs are everything to the Santas." Which makes what I did even worse. I'm such a ninny. I risked all those good children who hold onto those dreams losing their beliefs.

"I don't know what you did to get the boot, and I hope you don't repeat whatever those mistakes were, but there is one key point you're missing here." Sandy, Monty's mother as I'd recently learned her name, watched and waited for the lightbulb moment. When it didn't come she finished her thought. "Santa helped you find your mate. Many spend their entire life searching for that, but you were dropped in the lap of yours."

Huh. Never pictured me with a mate before.

"Now I know my Monty isn't the easiest to get along with. Nor the most outgoing, but I promise you my boy has a heart of gold. Once you get him out of bed." She shook her head. "Even as a baby he slept more than we did. First time I mentioned it to the doctor he laughed and said that boy had more bear than human in him."

"He hates me."

"Hate is a strong word, sweetie. Monty is not a people person but when it comes to family, he's there wherever and whenever he's needed. When Seth and Emmy's roof nearly came off during a storm, Monty braved the weather and did most of the repair work himself. He built this cabin with his own two hands. Stayed in a tent while he did it,"

Again with the head shake. "That boy is a stubborn one but when he cares he cares with his whole heart."

How do you mate with someone you don't know?

Someone so grouchy?

This was like one of those arranged marriages we'd all heard about.

"I've made such a mess."

"How so?"

"How can you start a relationship when you're literally thrown at someone?"

"Give it time, sweet boy. The two of you will find your groove, it just takes time."

Time.

Something I didn't have according to Santa's letter.

"Come on, let's get the boys to bring your stuff back so you can settle in. We've meddled enough tonight."

"Can I um, just have a minute to myself, please?" If that sounded rude, it wasn't my intention. I just wanted to catch my breath and rinse my face. Put on a bit of lip gloss too, that always made me feel better. Or at least it had in the past.

At this point, I had no clue who I was anymore. How quickly things had turned upside down. What I once thought was temporary I now knew was permanent.

"Will do but give me a hug first."

I loved hugs just as much as the next elf though they were few and far between for me, but this one felt...different. It wasn't forced or expected, it didn't have a two second limit. Sandy let me stay in her arms until I was the one who pulled away first.

She brushed the hair on my forehead aside. "I can't speak to your past, Twinkle, but you have a family now. Let us be there to help you."

I'd always been a loner. No friends, no real family. I never went out of my way to join my fellow elves in after-hours festivities or parties. Ultimately, I'd done this to myself and had no one else to blame for it. If that meant I spent the rest of my years in a loveless relationship, then so be it.

That was my punishment.

Could be worse.

Probably.

At least the house was clean now. Guess I found one thing I was good at other than annoying people.

Something in the air shifted as I emerged from the room. Voices that had filled it were now silent. I was center stage in a play I hadn't rehearsed for. I had no answers for myself, let alone for any of them and was thankful when Sandy took charge.

"Boys, why don't you take Twinkle's boxes to his room." At Sandy's order, Monty, Kody, Seth, and Joe picked up the packages and moved them in a single trip. When they returned, everyone said their goodbyes and I retreated to my new room to lick my wounds.

I plopped down on the floor and stared at the pile of boxes. With a heavy sigh, I resigned myself to the task at hand. "Might as well unpack. I've got no place else to go since no one wants me." Monty got stuck with me, though I neglected to say those words aloud. Thinking them was hard enough.

"Well," Monty's unexpected response as he came into the room made me jump. "Sorry, but I wouldn't say that." He handed me a cup.

"You made me cocoa?" No one ever made me cocoa. I always had to get my own. Had to admit the sweet gesture made my hopeful heart dance.

"Yes, first time making it, so you'll have to tell me if it's edible."

I feared the smile I gave came across as more of a grimace. "Ooh, tiny marshmallows." That made his debut creation appear a bit less scary. Slowly, I tilted the cup toward my lips and sipped. "Mmm, nummy and it's got a kick to it." I took another sip. I'd never had spicy hot cocoa, and I looked forward to another cup of the spicy chocolatey heaven.

"The secret ingredient is cayenne pepper." Monty was pleased with himself, as he should be.

"It's quite a delightful change. Thank you."

"Well," Monty cleared his throat, obviously as uncomfortable as I was. "I'll um, I'll let you get settled. Help yourself to whatever you need. Make a list of anything missing and maybe we can make it into town in a few days to pick it up for you."

"Thank you." With a nod, he left, and I was once again alone and lost to my thoughts. I didn't want to read too much into it. He was probably just being nice, but his olive branch was very welcome.

When I first got here, and while Monty napped, instead of trying to figure out what to do to in order to get back home or call out to Santa and ask, not that he would've responded, instead dove into what I do best. In typical Twinkle fashion I made Monty's home habitable—by my standard and without asking. Of course, he was asleep, but I just couldn't leave things alone. I didn't care what he thought or that this house and everything in it was his. I didn't focus on not having any of my things, honestly, I thought this whole ordeal was a joke and Santa twenty-seven would come and get me in a few days. Now that the truth had been revealed, it was a real game changer.

I was no longer Twinkle the elf.

The way I saw it I had two choices. Become Twinkle, the bear's mate, or forever be Twinkle the statue.

On the upside, if I chose Monty I'd no longer be alone. I wasn't sure if that was good or bad, but this harsh reality check had messed with my head and had me questioning everything I'd known about myself.

Was I really such a horrible elf that banishing me from my home was warranted?

Better yet, would anyone even miss me?

I cried myself to sleep on the tattered stuffie I'd found in the closet and had claimed as my own.

When I woke the next morning the urge to get up and start the day wasn't there. Normally, I woke with the sunrise, made breakfast and was off to work. Much the same had been done the few days I'd been here. Now I had to figure out a new norm. Do I cook breakfast for us both? Do I look for a job? I literally had zero useful skills outside the North Pole.

I could either lie here and fill my head full of what ifs or get up and find the answers.

Guess the day should begin with unboxing since I barely got through one last night before embarking upon my pity party for one. As I flung back the covers, fully expecting to see the elf uniform I'd fallen asleep in, it was instead...

"Santa. Flannel. Really?"

Now I feared what clothing awaited inside those boxes. The worst was confirmed as I opened the first one. "Flannel. Sweats. Jeans. Oh yay, hiking boots." The boots sent me into a tear-filled frenzy. How much worse could this get? I mean, really. Did I look like a boots and flannel kind of guy?

"What's wrong?" Monty burst into the room. "Twinkle, what happened?"

I was at a loss for words and pointed to the clothes strewn around me and grabbed my ears. "My ears are gone!"

"Twinkle, I thought you were hurt. What's going on?" Monty tugged on his beard as he sat on the floor beside me. "And your ears are there, they're just no longer pointy."

"Look at these clothes? Santa took away all my elf uniforms and replaced them with these!" I cried as I held the horrid garments up. "Does this look like something I'd wear?"

"Honestly, I don't know and while I don't see anything wrong with them it's an easy fix. We can order you new clothes or you could, I don't know, bedazzle them? Isn't that one of those shiny sparkly things?"

"I remember those. Santas gave them out in the nineties." Could I find one? "The boots and jeans wouldn't be half bad that way but these flannel tops and sweats. Seriously, no." Okay, my inner Diva had arrived.

"Why don't you shower and meet me in the kitchen, and we'll see what we can find online. Anything we order will be delivered to the post office in town and we'll have to pick it up, but it shouldn't take long. Give or take a winter storm or two. Do you need help hanging stuff up?"

Did I need help? Only with burning it.

"No thanks."

Monty let me be while I got to work. When my stomach growled I headed to the kitchen.

"Come on, have a seat." Monty had a cup of cocoa ready for me and had set a plate of food in front of me as I sat. "I know my opinion doesn't count, but I think you look good in flannel."

"I wish I saw what you saw but it's a no for me." I was sparkly, shiny and I liked to twinkle like my namesake. With a healthy side of attitude. That was who I was. "I need to get a job, but I don't have any real world skills."

"That's a worry for another day. Let's get you what you need first and take it from there. You've had a lot thrown at you in a short period and you need time to absorb it and find your place."

"Do you have a job?"

"I do though I don't do much work during the winter months outside of emergencies. I'm a contractor and I do a lot of jobs in town as well as up here on the mountain."

"That makes sense. Your mom told me you built this house."

Monty set his fork down and took a sip of coffee. "I did. Took a bit longer than I'd hoped. That was the summer we had a few nasty storms that caused a lot of damage in town, so my time was diverted. But I'm pleased with how it turned out. Thank you, by the way, for cleaning it up."

Guess he wasn't mad after all. "You're welcome. Sorry I didn't ask first."

"Well, it's your home now, too. If there's something you want to change or, I don't know, want frilly pillows or whatever, just let me know."

Shocked didn't even cover how I felt. Grouchy Monty was doing his best to be amiable. Even if his eye twitched while doing so. "You really wouldn't mind if I," I glanced around the living room, "brightened things up?"

"Considering you already did with the Twinkle lights." *Wait, was that a grin?* "I'd say you were well on your way to redecorating."

"Yeah, but that was before..." Before what? He got stuck with me. We got notified in front of his entire family we were mates.

Monty cleared his throat. "Twinkle, neither of us knew about the mate thing. Hell, I'd resigned long ago I'd be alone forever. This is as much a surprise to me as it is to you."

"Only difference was you have a home, and I was taken from mine."

Was it considered kidnapping if Santa himself did it?

"This is your home now, Twinkle. We move at our pace and in our own time. Sort of."

That one major piece hung in the air between us. There was only one way to mate and there was no way around that part of the deal.

Ugh, reindeer pooh!

"You look like you just swallowed needles. What's going on in the head of yours?"

"Just the um, you know." I swirled my finger around as though that made complete and total sense and explained everything.

"I don't follow."

There was no way he could because I made exactly zero sense.

"The um, the." *Deep breath, Twinkle.* "Mating thing."

"Mating thing?"

"I've um, never mated before."

"Of course you haven't. Mating is for life."

He wasn't getting it. Red-faced or not, this was something he should know. "No, I mean I haven't *m-a-t-e-d*," I spelled the word out. "Ever."

When the meaning hit Monty, he blushed. "Okay, good to know. How did you handle heats before?"

"We had pills we took. Our lives revolved around the Santa's we served, and missing work was bad for us. It set us way back in production if we did plus everyone loved their jobs. We never got sick, only took vacations when the Santas told us to. Maternity leave was scheduled, really everything was scheduled in our lives." Saying it aloud was exhausting. How had we survived the go-go-go of our daily regimented routines?

"Wow, that's a lot."

"That would definitely reduce your nap time."

"There he is, the snarky Twinkle from the box."

My turn to blush, he made me sound like the latest and greatest new toy. Maybe when you found your mate they turned out to be the one who got who you truly were. What others disliked about me Monty appeared to enjoy. Now to find a balance so I didn't push him away by being...me.

"Come on, let's clean up and then get to shopping."

Working as a team was quite empowering and we had the kitchen in order in no time.

"Okay, take a seat beside me and I'll show you what we've got."

How close should I get? How close was too close? If our legs touched, would he pull away?

"Deep breath, Twinkle. I don't bite, unsolicited at least," Monty winked, and it did something silly to my insides. "Besides, you can't see the screen from way over there."

Monty sat on the center cushion which did nothing to narrow down my seating selection. Finally, having overthought this far too much, I sat.

"Okay. Do you know your sizes?"

"No. Taylor had all that information back at the North Pole. He and his elves made all our uniforms." Elves ran every aspect of our lives.

"Here's my thoughts. Keep the clothes you've got,"

When I began to protest he held up a hand.

"Hear me out. There will undoubtedly come a time when you'll need them, boots included. So um, I wouldn't bedazzle all of it."

I giggled, Monty's face was equal parts humor and horror. Guess he wasn't a bedazzle kind of guy. "Understood."

"When we go into town to pick up the new orders, we can browse through the shops there as well. At least then you can try stuff on first and see how it fits. Though now that I think about it, wouldn't the clothes and the boots he left you have a size in them? Here, turn around." Monty pulled on the back collar of my shirt then checked the waist of my pants and I took off one of my shoes. "Perfect. Let me plug the sizes in."

Monty handed me the computer. "Just grab a couple of things that catch your eye. Not sure if he left you any boxers but grab those if you need them too. I'd offer my clothes to you, but you'd swim in them."

He was a tall, muscular man, and I wondered how big his bear was. Was it black or brown? Was he eight feet tall with big, long teeth and huge claws?

"What are you thinking about over there besides all those bright, shiny colors you put into the cart?"

When had he gotten up?

"Done." I handed the laptop back for him to finish the checkout process.

"Alright, everything should be here in a couple of days. Now, back to my question."

Time to take charge and knock this timid Twinkle to the side. "Can I see your bear? Is he big? Ooohhh I bet he's furry with a big growl. Rawr!" I did a ridiculous impression of a bear but with Monty smiling at me like he was that made it fun. That smile of his, it just did something to me, and I came alive. Next thing I knew I was bouncing up and down on the couch.

"Okay, okay, let's not break anything. Namely, you." Monty watched as I sat on my hands to keep from fidgeting. "You are gonna be a handful, aren't you?"

Maybe...

"I'll do this, but I have to get naked in order to shift or I'll shred my clothes. Are you okay with that?"

Was I?

Chapter Four
Monty

As much as Twinkle wanted to meet my bear, I wasn't sold that he was prepared to see my naked ass in the process. Clarity, communication, and holding my temper in check would be the key to winning him over and keeping him from freaking out. Not gonna lie, when I read that letter from Santa aloud and learned he was my mate my heart skipped several beats. Had the way I'd viewed Twinkle up until then changed? Yes, and without my forcing it to.

Winning him over. Who was I and what happened to grouchy Monty?

Freaking Santa. I didn't know whether to hug or punch him.

Twinkle's head bobbed up and down. "Yes, I'm good with that. Can I touch you when you're a bear? Can you talk? Can you understand me when I talk to you?"

I'd never smiled more in my life than I had today. His rapid-fire questions were like a breath of fresh air or in his case, fired off in a single burst of air. "Yes you can touch me. No, I can't speak human words. I can only communicate with other bears telepathically. Yes I can understand you. Did I miss anything?"

I wondered if I could communicate with my mate through a mental connection as I did with other bears.

"Nope, nope." Twinkle popped up and grabbed my hand and tried to pull me along. "Let's go. I wanna play with Monty bear."

"Monty bear?"

"Yes, my Monty bear."

His Monty bear. I was definitely on the path to being just that. How fast was too fast when you knew it was your mate?

"We need to go outside, or I'll wreck the house." Controlling paws and claws was a hell of a lot harder than hands and feet were while tucked into small spaces.

Just inside the door, I removed my clothes and glanced up at Twinkle. His curious gaze was glued to me as he took in my entire...package. It was one of those moments where your ego puffed up and you couldn't stop yourself from drawing it out and turning it into a bit of a show. In bear years, I was in my prime and between being a shifter and working manual labor I was in damn good shape.

By the time I was gloriously naked, a red-faced Twinkle stood before me with his hands covering his crotch.

"You alright there, Twinkle?" A little flirting was in order, at least I felt it was. Hell, I stood before my mate fully naked and rock hard myself. To shift in this state would not be wise so thoughts of less arousing scenarios were required.

"Does it, does it hurt when you shift?" He stuttered as we stepped outside.

I shrugged. "In the beginning more so than it does now. When you're young you're excited for the first one until the bones pop out of place. Then you turn into a screaming banshee. Once you learn to control the shift rather than having it control you the faster and less painful it becomes. Well, mostly painless but tolerable. It's worth it to have the freedom I feel while in my bear form. My soul is more settled and there's a sense of freedom that comes along with it."

"Sounds scary. You don't have to do it, forget I asked."

His adorable reply, oh my Goddess, did I really just think the word adorable? That stopped me dead from taking his hands in mine. Instead, I did something else equally as uncharacteristic of me, unless I was playing with the little ones, and shifted a single ear. Twinkle's eyes widened as it returned to human form, so I shifted to the other. Back and forth I went. His eyes bounced along with the changes and his smile widened which made the ridiculous game more than worth it.

"That is so neat!" He clapped and cheered. "More!"

Before his eyes, Monty the bear appeared in full form. Twinkle jumped and squealed and clapped some more. Had anyone ever been this excited to see my bear?

That was easy to answer–no.

"Monty, you're beautiful! Can I touch you?" I dropped to the ground and lowered my head, so it was within reach. "You are so soft. You're like a big furry rug I want to roll all over."

A rug? I huffed.

"Don't you huff at me." Twinkle shook a scolding finger.

Back to that word *adorable* as the tiny human believed he was in charge.

"Have you ever had a fuzzy, super soft rug before? It's like getting a stocking stuffed full of all your favorite things. Squishy under your feet and body when you roll around on it."

I swear, the little guy purred.

"I wonder if Santa knew what he was doing?"

I cocked my head and wondered what he was getting at.

"I never had a bear stuffie of my own and now he brought me a real one."

Did you hear that crack?

Might've been a stress fracture in the brick wall I hid my heart behind.

"Okay, Mr. Bear, show me what you can do."

What could I do? Not much other than forage for berries and sleep. Oh, and protect the ones I loved though battles were few and far between, thankfully. Scared off a few wolves here and there trying to get into my brother Seth's chicken coop. Not a fan of fighting, personally, but I'd do whatever it took to protect those I loved.

Ssshhh, don't let them know.

I wracked my brain for anything fun and exciting to show Twinkle but all I could come up with was to carry him and run around. I picked Twinkle up and finagled him into place like a backpack. He wrapped his arms around my neck and shouted, "Go Beary, go!"

I guess I was Beary now...

It was oddly satisfying as we traipsed through the snow. Twinkle's giggles echoed around the forest filling the air with much needed laughter. Goddess, if anyone saw us like this I'd never hear the end of it but for the first time, I couldn't bring myself to care.

Round and round we went, through the trees, around the fencing that contained my summer garden. I harvested many of the fruits and vegetables I ate year-round from it, beyond thankful for the fertile soil for which it was built it upon. Momma canned much of it to store for winter months and shared it amongst the family as my brothers and sisters did with their gardens and the eggs from their coops.

Blessed by the Goddess herself, I was. How had I never realized this before.

Too busy living inside your own damn head...

I bucked Twinkle off, and he landed in a nearby snow drift, giggling like mad. I pressed my muzzle to his belly, extracting more laughter, and continued playing with him. When he'd had enough he lay back against the snow, smiling up at me so sweetly it stole my breath. Twinkle truly was a vision and a beautiful one at that. In a sudden move, the minx lifted his head, pressed his lips to my snout and took off toward the house and left me...

Stunned. Confused. Breathless.

All of the above.

And also, tired. That was a hell of a workout.

I ran back toward the house and shifted just off the front porch. "Brr." I shivered and hurriedly stepped inside. Twinkle was there waiting with my bathrobe. "Thank you."

He twirled, something I'd learned he did when happy. "That was so much fun. Best day ever!"

Twinkle had no idea how that made me feel. Maybe one day when I was more comfortable with us, I'd tell him. "Is that food I smell?"

"Yes, I thought you might be hungry after all that exercise." A yawn escaped right on queue. "And tired. Let's get food into my Beary before he sleeps away the wintery days."

His Beary.

Why did hearing that make my heart race? Hell, why had everything Twinkle-related do that?

"Do I have time for a quick shower?" I may no longer be shifted but I still smelled like I was.

"Absolutely. Shower away!" Twinkle spun again and stirred whatever was in the pot as I headed down the hall toward my room. Christmas music came on as I shut the door, and he sang along with it. Here it was January, and I wondered if these holly jolly tunes would become a year-round fixture in our home.

Our home.

How odd was it to think that? Numerous reality checks hit me today and yet none of them gave me the urge to run. Momentarily pause, yes, but running never once crossed my mind.

"Nap, Monty. You need food and a nap." A long, long one at that. Time to recharge and clear my head. How far away was spring?

Hurriedly, I washed with the forethought of eating and going right to bed. But a cheerful Twinkle held my attention longer than anticipated throughout dinner as he chattered way.

"I had so much fun today. When can we do it again?" He wiggled his little butt in the chair. "Your bear is stunning!"

Gush-gush. "Well, Twinkle, I can promise you that we will but for now this old bear needs a nap." His face dimmed, but a second later brightened. Was that a strong façade he put up for me by trying not to show he wasn't ready for this day to come to an end? Would there ever come a time where I didn't feel the need to nap as much as I did now? I sincerely hoped so.

"Thank you for dinner, Twinkle, you're a wonderful cook." I rose and grabbed the plates and he joined me in the kitchen for clean-up.

"Honestly, I found this in your freezer and heated it up. I couldn't even tell you what it was let alone what was in it, but it was nummy." His word choices cracked me up. He'd not uttered a single curse word thus far.

"Ah, probably something Momma put together and froze. Believe it or not, I can cook but she is so used to cooking for the entire family that even once we left the den she kept cooking enough for an army."

Twinkle snickered.

"Once we all moved out of the house, she kept cooking enough to feed the pack. She gets bored, cooks then delivers it to each of us kids. I don't mind, Momma's a great cook and it's like being home again."

"Where do we get groceries? Is it like at the North Pole, we just place an order, and it appears a few minutes later?"

Wow, life where Twinkle came from was a hell of a lot simpler. "No, what we can't grow we buy in town. The fencing you saw outside today," he nodded, "that's my garden. Come summer it'll be packed full of berries and vegetables. Meats and such we hunt or buy." His eyes widened and his face paled. "Are you okay, Twinkle?"

"I-I ate an animal?"

"Yes, what did you think you were eating?"

"I didn't know it was meat!" Twinkle burst into tears and all sense of keeping my distance fell away as I scooped the crying elf up and tucked him tightly against me.

"Oh, honey." I carried him over to the couch and sat and cradled him on my lap. "I'm so sorry, I thought you knew." I dared not tell him which animals he consumed, or I'd be investing in therapy for the poor guy based upon this reaction. "Are you Vegan or Vegetarian?"

"I, I, I don't know." He stumbled over his words. "I ate everything the chefs made, but we never had meat. Elves don't kill."

"What about fish and seafood?"

"Oh yes." He popped up and faced me. "Shrimps are nummy-nummy."

"Okay, that makes you a Pescatarian. I'll have Momma start marking the containers she brings over and then we will know which is which. Have you ever been fishing?" I loved to fish though I didn't use a pole. Nothing like trapping the floppy fish in your jowls.

"I've never been fishing but if you like it I'll try it. Just please, don't ever ask me to kill Bambi or Thumper. Or even Clarabelle and Clarence."

I knew what animals the first two were and I was guessing the last two were cows but would confirm via Google later. "Absolutely, sweetie." Ah, two pet names had made a break for it. Damn my lack of filter. "What can I do to make this better?"

"Just hold me," Twinkle snuggled in, his head tucked against my shoulder. "This is nice."

Yes, yes it was indeed.

Twinkle and I dozed off on the couch. His merry tunes lulled us into slumber though when I woke, Twinkle was nowhere to be found.

"Twinkle?" My back and neck popped as I stretched. I heard his sweet singing coming from his room and followed it there. In the center of the bed sat Twinkle, dressed in his new snowmen pajamas and singing carols to my old bear.

"There you are." He smiled up at me. The creek of the door gave my stalking away. "You've been asleep forever."

Such a drama major. "Forever huh?" But when I looked around I realized there wasn't much for Twinkle to entertain himself with when I did sleep or was away at work. "What kinds of things do you like to do for fun, Twinkle?"

His face lit up like I'd asked the million-dollar question. "I like to make snow angels, build gingerbread houses, wrap presents. Well, when the gift wrap elves let me. Decorating the tree is the best fun ever!"

Alright, nothing I had on hand for sure.

"What about movies? Have you watched anything new on the streaming services I have?"

"No," he sighed. "I've just never really been into TV unless it's Christmas shows."

"Okay, what about..." I wracked my brain for anything fun. "Do you like to color or paint? Maybe do puzzles."

"Oh yes, all of those things."

Now we were getting somewhere. "Why don't we order you some, maybe a few other crafty goodies so you're not bored while I sleep."

"That would be so nice. I'm really looking forward to planting a garden. I've never seen one before. It snows at the North Pole year-round. Have you ever built a snowman? It's so much fun."

Why had I begun to believe elves were more childlike than I'd imagined. Or maybe only mine was.

"Come on, Twinkle, let's get to ordering."

Twinkle skipped down the hall behind me, whistling a catchy tune I couldn't quite make out. Likely something jolly. I sat, laptop in place and he stood there staring at me. He wiggled his butt, grinned, picked up the laptop and replaced it with his bottom atop my lap and held the computer on his.

"My new seat."

I kissed the top of his head, and his smile widened.

"Let's get to it."

Twinkle pointed to a variety of items, during which we lost track of time as he chatted away.

"Maybe if I'm good, Santa will bring me a stuffie this year that looks like Monty Beary."

That shot straight to my heart and gave me an idea. As soon as I put my sleepy elf to bed, I'd order a variety of goodies to surprise him with.

"All right, sleepy head." I must've slept longer than I thought if he was already tired.

Twinkle yawned again, "let's get you tucked in."

"Carry me." Twinkle threw his arms around my neck. I swung him over my shoulder and carried him fireman style. He laughed and broke into a fit of giggles when I dropped him on the bed. "That was fun."

Twinkle crawled under the blankets, and I tucked them in around him and pressed my lips to his forehead. "Goodnight Twinkle."

"Goodnight, my bear."

Chapter Five

TWINKIE

"This is fun." Monty Bear and I were driving into town to pick up all our online orders. Again. This was the second trip of this nature and I thoroughly enjoyed it.

"You're only happy because you get gifts." He winked at me then returned his gaze to the road ahead. If I didn't know better, and I likely didn't, I'd think he was flirting with me which was fun too. Most everything was fun with Monty involved. He made all the sad thoughts go away.

"You're like a little excitable pup, Twinkle."

Blink-blink.

"Can we get a puppy?" I'd never had a pet before and the thought of a prospective puppy was exciting. I literally bounced as much as the seatbelt would allow. Stupid seatbelt.

"Probably not a bad idea though he or she may not like my bear. I'd heard instances of it not working out, mixing species, but my brothers have had dogs without issue."

"Can we look? Is there a pet place in town? How do you get one? Ohhhh!"

Monty laughed. "Okay, down boy. Pet stores and local breeders are how most get theirs though I'd prefer to rescue a lost soul from a shelter. Let's get our errands run then we can stop there on the way home. Can you make it that long?"

Lost soul, just like me. "Yes, please and thank you."

"Morning Monty, morning, Twinkle," Mr. Benjamin at the post office greeted us. "Have a few packages for you."

"Morning, Ben. Yes, getting Twinkle all set up." For as grouchy as Monty bear was, he was nice to Mr. Benjamin. And to me, actually.

"Monty, how much did we order?" Mr. Benjamin came around the corner with a big mail cart packed full of packages. "Are all of those ours?"

Mr. Benjamin laughed. "They're got your name and address on them. Well, Monty's but I'm sure they're for you."

"I may've gone a bit overboard." Monty shrugged.

Monty bear was so silly. Who knew what all those boxes held. It was like Christmas for Twinkle. Now I am excited for the giant unboxing ceremony.

"Fizzle sticks."

"What's wrong, Twinkle?" My near curse words as Monty finished loading the truck startled him. "Did we forget something?"

"Where will we put the puppy?"

Mr. Benjamin glanced at Monty, then into the truck and back to me. "Did we trap a pup beneath the boxes?"

Monty shook his head. "No, Ben. I promised Twinkle we'd go to the shelter and look at pups on the way home."

"Good Lord, Twinkle. You nearly gave this old man a heart attack."

"Sorry, Mr. Benjamin." Not sure what I did exactly, but that felt like the appropriate response.

"Thanks for your help, Ben." Monty shut the gate on the truck. "Hop in, Twinkle. We have a couple more stops."

I wanted to scream, kick, and throw a fit about all the stops, but I wanted a puppy more, so I kept the bad behavior in check. First time for everything. Huh, maybe with the new year came a new Twinkle.

"I see you stewing over there, Twinkle. Be good."

That's twice he'd said that now and I wondered if he considered me to be the new puppy.

We passed by what I thought was our next stop. "Don't we have to go to that big food store place?"

Monty laughed. "The grocery store and we do but I figured if we didn't get this stop out of the way you might snap."

We drove to the edge of town and parked in front of a barn. A few other cars were there, and I saw some horses behind a fence. "Horses Monty, look! Can we pet them?" They weren't as big as Santa's reindeer, but they were way bigger than me.

"Come on." Monty hopped out and I followed him over to the horses.

"They're so pretty. We should've brought carrots." I petted the long nose on the brown and white spotted one. "Such a pretty pony."

"Actually, they prefer apples." Some guy said as he walked up, Monty growled beside me, and I wondered what that was for.

"Clint."

"Monty. Who's this?"

Monty wrapped an arm around my waist and tucked me into his side. "My mate, Twinkle."

"Ah, I see. Nice to meet you, Twinkle."

I wasn't sure how to respond or even if I should given how stiff Monty became with this guy near. The smile Monty had when we walked up was gone, replaced by the growly Monty I first met.

"What brings you out this way, Monty?"

Monty growled again and was about to sputter a few curse words.

I put my hand on his chest to stop him. "We're getting a puppy."

"Awe isn't that nice. Look at Monty all domesticated and shit."

Oh, I didn't like this guy at all, picking on my Monty Bear.

"Come on, Monty, let's go." I didn't know where this puppy place was, but it was time to leave.

I took his hand and tugged him toward the truck, but he stopped at the walkway that led to the big red and white barn. "Let's go inside."

I shrugged and followed him. Besides, he still had ahold of my hand.

As soon as Monty opened the door I was in heaven. The air was filled with happy barks, puppies on leashes with humans leading them. I jumped and squealed, the puppies turned toward me, and I ran to each one to pet them.

"Twinkle, you need to approach strange dogs slowly, so they don't see you as a threat." Monty warned, but I was too far gone to have my own leash tugged. "And also ask permission of their handler first."

"Sorry Monty, but they like me." The silly brown and white one licked my face, and I giggled. "He's so happy."

"He is actually a she and her name is Jazzy, and we just adopted her." The lady holding her leash said.

"She's so beautiful. Jazzy will make you so happy, I just know it. You're such a sweet girl, Jazzy." I kissed her nose and moved along to another pup while Monty talked to the lady at the desk. "I hope there are more for us."

"Sadly, there are but it's been a good day. I'm Marla, the manager here at Kodiak Rescue."

"Marla it's wonderful to meet you, I'm Twinkle, Monty's mate." That was the first time I said it, and it was just as fun to say as it was to hear that word from Monty.

Marla smiled at me. "Follow me, Twinkle and we'll show you around."

"Kitties!" There was a big wall of glass and behind it was like a thousand cats climbing all over their climby things. "Look at all the kitties, Monty."

"Yes," Marla smiled. "That is our cat condo room. Every cat in that room is looking for their forever home too."

"Monty, kitties need a home too." I was sad for the kitties even though they appeared to be having fun.

"Let's start with a pup first, okay?"

"'Kay."

We followed Marla back through a heavy metal door and past a big tub. "This is one of three bathing areas we have for the animals."

As soon as we walked through the second door, the barking hit me full on and I froze.

"Everything okay, Twinkle?" Monty stopped beside me. Concern marred his handsome face.

"That's a lot of dogs. Big dogs, small dogs, medium dogs. That's a lot of dogs. And they all need homes?" I was so sad for them. How awful it must be to not have a warm bed of your own.

"Yes, Twinkle," Marla replied. "They are all hoping to find their forever homes."

"Monty?" I was on the verge of tears, I felt so bad for them.

"We can only take one, Twinkle. I'm sorry." Monty's hand rubbed soothing circles along my back and while I was still sad, it was nice when he touched me.

Cage by cage we walked, letting the dogs who met me at each gate sniff my hand like Monty and Marla showed me. It tickled when they licked my hand, and I petted their heads to thank them for their kisses. Monty stayed back. He didn't want his bear scent to upset them though some still growled at him.

"Do you see any you want to meet?" Marla asked me. "We have a meet and greet area where you can interact with them."

"I can?" I nearly danced at the thought. "What about this one?" I pointed to a pretty girl. The name on the paper outside the cage read Tina. "Tina."

"She's a sweet girl. Tina is an Australian Shepherd mix. They're herding dogs." Marla slid a leash around Tina's neck. "Follow me."

Monty and I followed her to a nearby office, once inside, she shut the door and removed Tina's leash. "There are some toys in that basket if you want to play with her."

I grabbed a ball and tossed it. Tina barked and chased after it. "Look Monty, she got the ball!"

"Yes, she's good at fetching but not so much with returning it to you." Monty smiled fondly at us. "But I bet she's a fast learner."

Tina and I went back and forth like this for I don't know how long. It was gonna take a while to get her used to bringing it back to me like Monty said but training will be fun.

"Treats as rewards while training will go over well," Marla told us.

"Good to know, we'll stock up for sure."

Monty and Marla talked about boring stuff while Tina and I played tug of war with a rope toy that was in the basket. This was so much fun. For the first time I had a real friend.

"I want Tina, Monty. What do you think?" *Please say yes. Please say yes.*

"Well, let me see if she'll come to me, or if she backs away and growls." Until this point, Monty had kept his distance, talking with Marla while Tina and I played.

Slowly, he came toward her. When he neared, he dropped onto one knee and held his hand out for her to sniff. Tina stilled and turned her head from side to side, it was the cutest thing ever. Then she got up and trotted right over to him and licked his hand.

"Are you sure it's Tina you want Twinkle?"

"Yes! Yes! Yes!" I clapped and jumped up and down.

"Ms. Marla, I think Tina will do just fine."

"Yay! Do we get to take her home now?"

Tina sat and Marla scratched between her ears. "We've got some paperwork to do, and you need to get food and a few other things before you can take her home. We have a pet supply store that's in the building next door where you can get all of that."

"Alright, Twinkle, while I fill out the paperwork, why don't you go next door and start shopping for our new girl. I'll meet you over there."

Our new girl. Those simple words filled me with joy like no other.

"Okay." I bent down and gave Tina one last pet, and she licked my face and I was back to giggling. "I'll be right back, sweet girl. I'm gonna go find all kinds of fun new stuff for you."

Monty moaned. "There goes my credit card."

Marla laughed. "It'll be more than worth it with the way Twinkles face lit up."

"I think you found him the perfect pup."

"Yes, I believe we did."

"Twinkle, if you go out the front door and turn right, you'll see a big sign that says, Kodiak Pet Store. Monty and I will meet you over there. I think you'll find everything you need to get your girl started and Sarah can help you find her food, just give her this piece of paper." Marla handed me a page with Tina's information on it. "And she'll know exactly what you need."

"Perfect," I stood on tippy toes and kissed Monty's cheek.

"Thank you, Marla." On that note, I skipped out the door and down the hall.

"Whoa," I said, as I stepped outside and spotted the store. "This place is ginormous."

A woman greeted me as I stepped inside. "Welcome. I'm Sarah how can I help?" My eyes were wide, taking it all in.

"I'm getting a puppy. Marla said to give you this paper and you'd be able to help me get everything my new girl Tina needs."

Sarah smiled and took the paper from me. You'd have thought I ate all the candy canes in Santa's bag with as excited as I was.

"That's correct, let's get to work. While I pull out the food and treats that are healthy for her, why don't you find a pretty new collar and leash and then we can use the machine over there to make her tags." She pointed to something that looked like a video game. "Maybe pick out a couple of toys for her. Do you know if you're going to kennel train?"

"Oh, I don't think we'll need to because I'll be home with her all the time. She'll probably go everywhere with me." I couldn't wait to put on her cute little winter coat and go for walks and make puppy snow angels.

"Okay, no worries," Sarah said.

"Can puppies have cookies?"

"Only specific dog approved ones. There are some over with the snacks, even a mix and match area where you can pick out different ones."

"Yay!"

After I filled a bag with lots of pretty cookies, I wandered from shelf to shelf. There were so many cute things to buy. Another guy who worked here brought me a basket to put the pile I was struggling with carrying into. I picked Tina the cutest pink collar with rainbows on it and a matching leash. There were so many great toys to choose from, even I wanted to play with them. I guess I kind of would be when I played with Tina. There, we could share. Problem solved.

The squeaky hamburger was an instant favorite. I squeaked it as I walked around, kind of turned it into a beat I danced to.

"I should have known you'd find the noisiest toy in the place." Monty's voice startled me but did nothing to wipe the smile off my face.

I glanced behind him. "Where's Tina?"

"She's with Marla. They had to give her a couple shots. Good news is she's already been spayed, so we don't have to worry about that. They're cleaning her up and getting her ready to go for you. As soon as we buy what she needs we'll load her up and hit the grocery store on the way home." Monty took the basket, but I held onto the hamburger.

"Are we allowed to take her into the big food store?" I didn't know what the rules were and causing any more trouble wasn't high on my list of wants any longer. Lesson learned and all that.

"Well," Sarah said as she walked up, "in some towns it's frowned upon but lucky for us the folks in Kodiak are lenient and animal lovers." She winked at Monty. "They just ask that you not take them into the restaurant kitchens. On the outside patio they have water dishes for the dogs and treats as well."

"That is so cool. I love Tina already, and I don't ever want to be away from her. Now she can go everywhere Monty and I go." I'd quickly warmed up to my new life, but this really sealed the deal for me. Not that I had a choice, but it was nice to be happy just the same.

Monty smiled at me. "That's the plan, Twinkle. Occasionally we might go somewhere that she can't but that'll be rare. I always wanted the kind of dog that I could take on job sites with me and if you go, it'll be a family affair."

Family.

Twinkle the lonely elf had a family of his own.

Finally.

I couldn't wait for everything Monty mentioned to happen. I was excited for our new life though I wasn't sure where I fit in. Yet. Maybe he had special jobs lined up for me. I was a great helper and a fast learner. Even though I pretty much always made everybody mad. But so far this this life wasn't as lonely as my old one and I had no desire to cook up trouble to get attention. I only hoped it stayed that way.

No more naughty Twinkle.

Sarah rang everything up and Monty slid a card through that little machine on the counter. I'd learned much in the time I'd been here but still had a long way to go. I supposed if I needed to know how something worked that Monty would explain it to me.

"Here Twinkle, take the leash and collar so you can put it on Tina. I made the tag with all our information and attached it already. Let's put the bags in the truck and go get our girl."

"Yay!"

When we walked back inside the big building were the animals were, Tina was waiting for us by the front desk with Marla. As soon as she saw me her little nub of a tail bobbed up and down. She was just as excited to see me as I was to see her.

"Did Sarah get you guys taken care of?" Marla asked.

"Yes." Monty bent to pet Tina. "Sarah took very good care of my credit card."

"She was wonderful. We got so many new things for our girl. I just know that Tina will be happy with us. Look, we got a new collar and a leash. Aren't they cute?" I held them up and the tag jingled.

"They are very cute and perfect for her. Let me show you the proper way to fit a collar." Marla put it around Tina's neck, and I watched as she measured which hole to put the silver thingy in and latched it in place. "See how I can fit a finger underneath this collar?" I nodded. "That's what you want. You want it so it's not too tight, so she can still breathe and move around but not so loose that it slides off over her head and she gets away."

"Oh, that would be very bad, and I'd be very sad." Just the thought caused my eyes to tear.

"Yes, we all would be. It's not safe for animals to run around loose. They can get hurt, or worse."

I didn't want to think about what Marla said. I knew it was true, but it was just too heartbreaking for me. I'd only just met Tina, and I was already in love with her. I couldn't imagine how the volunteers at the shelter would feel after being with the animals as much as they had. Bonds were formed whether you tried to distance your heart or not.

"Alright, I think you guys are ready to go." Marla handed me Tina's leash. "Monty, you have all the paperwork. If you have any questions, feel free to give us a call. She's had all her shots, and I put the card for the local veterinarian who also volunteers here so you can set up her follow up appointment. I'll transfer a copy of her records to him as well for you."

"Thank you for everything Marla." Monty and I shook Marla's hand. "Alright, Tina, are you ready to see your new home?" She barked right on queue. "I'll take that as a yes."

Tina rode on my lap all the way to the big food store, licking my face every once in a while like she was making sure I was still there. After Monty parked, we hopped out and followed him inside. She sniffed everything within reach along the way. I guess it was just as new to her as it was to me. Hurriedly, we gathered all the groceries off Monty's list and by the time we loaded those in the truck it was filled to the brim. But we were stocked up and ready to show our girl her new home.

Chapter Six
Monty

I shot off a text to my brothers though it might be a while before I heard back. Reception on our land was spotty at the best of times. Not only did I need to forewarn them we had a pup on site, but I was hopeful they'd lend me a hand with erecting a new fenced in area for Tina to roam freely.

"Twinkle, why don't you get Tina situated? Make sure to set up her water dish so it's out of the way and easy to clean around."

"Okay, Monty Bear."

Ah, so we were back to the whole Monty Bear thing. Had to admit, it'd grown on me just as Twinkle had. He could be sassy and snarky, but he had a huge heart and was excited with the simplest of things.

Twinkle danced across the room and stopped in front of me and threw his arms around my neck. This was our first embrace, and my arms itched to pull him against me. Sure, he'd taken up perching himself on my lap but we'd not full on hugged or so much as kissed.

"Thank you, Monty bear. I know I don't always say or do the right thing but I'm trying."

"I know you are, sweetheart. You weren't exactly given a choice in all of this but I'm doing my best to make you, correction, make us happy."

"You're succeeding." Twinkle pressed his lips to mine in a long-awaited kiss. Long awaited by me, that was. I'd thought about it for some time now but wasn't sure the best way to approach it. Goddess, how perfect he felt in my arms and now with the seal broken I'd take as many liberties as Twinkle would allow. Beginning with sliding my tongue between those slightly parted lips.

Twinkle froze, uncertain what to do as I tangled my tongue with his. A virgin in every sense of the word and he was all mine. I looked forward to testing the water, searching every nook and cranny on his body for those oh so sweet spots that made him purr. I'd take damn good care of Twinkle, Santa, I promise that.

"Wow," Twinkle whispered as we drew apart. "That was..." His face was red and when his erection hit mine he jumped back, embarrassed.

Tina circled us, barking and wagging her nub like mad. "Alright girl, I promise we haven't forgotten you." I stole another quick kiss and let Twinkle get to work. Meanwhile, I'd go cool off in my man cave. Take inventory of supplies, wait for my cock to simmer down. Those sorts of man cave things.

"Here Twinkle," I grabbed the box I knew was his special gift and handed it to him. "Open this."

He tore into it like a kid on Christmas day, ha, sometimes I made myself laugh.

"Squee!" he squealed. "You got me a Monty bear!"

"Yes, I did."

"I love it. Thank you so much."

Oddly enough, the damn bear looked exactly like me. The picture online didn't do it enough justice. It was even handsomer in person.

With the snow melting, the ground was soft enough that with a bit of effort, in the form of my brother Joe, the posts could be laid. I'd chosen the area just outside the back door since it was hardly used and got to work staking it out while I waited to hear from my brothers.

"She had an oopsie-daisy on the floor, but I cleaned it up." Twinkles' voice surprised me. "Sorry, didn't mean to scare you."

"No worries. If you take her out every couple of hours and praise her for doing her business outside, she'll catch on." Twinkle visibly relaxed. Had he required my praise for doing the right thing? I'd have to remember that.

"Okay, I can do that. What are you building?" Twinkle asked as Tina sniffed around as far as her leash would allow.

"Thought it would be nice for Tina to have her own safe space outside. With spring just around the corner she'll want to be outdoors more." At least, I assumed she did. As a bear I loved it once the weather was ideal and spent the majority of my time outside. The scent of the flowers in bloom, fresh berries plucked from the neighboring bushes. It was by far my favorite time of year.

"That is so sweet." I swear, Twinkle swooned. Can't say I'd ever had that effect on another and I ate it up. "How can I help?"

"While I appreciate the offer, I'm in my zone with this though I did send a shout out to Seth, Cody, and Joe for a helping hand."

Twinkle got a disappointed look in his eye. How quickly I went from being a winner to a loser.

"But I know something you can do for me." *Quick recovery, dumbass. Don't do it again.* "Besides training Tina, which is a huge job, would you mind figuring out dinner for us? We kind of skipped lunch today."

"Oh, yes, absolutely." Twinkle instantly brightened up. "I'm a good helper. I like to help."

That's all he wanted—to be included and not overlooked. Maybe Santa and the other elves missed that about him. Granted, mischief wasn't the best way to get noticed but I did understand Twinkle a bit better having figured this out.

Twinkle skipped inside with Tina hot on his heels. I'm sure in no time she'd likely do the same. The visual of a man and his dog, both skipping along. Sounded like the stuff children's storybooks were derived from.

"Hello brother of mine," I said to Kody as I answered his call.

"Putting up a fence for a new dog, huh? Who knew grouchy old Monty would ever be domesticated." The jackass laughed.

"Cute, smart ass. Twinkle wanted a puppy, and we went down to the shelter and found the perfect one for him. Sweet little gal, herding breed. Her name is Tina, and I decided to build her a private yard so she could run around and play without worry." Maybe Kody was right, though I'd never tell him that, but even my response came across as domesticated.

"Wow, if Mom gets wind of this she'll be planning your wedding."

"Goddess, don't get that woman started." I supposed that was inevitable given she knew Twinkle and I were mates. We kinda did this whole relationship thing a bit backwards. Santa's to blame for that one.

"Well, I'm all booked up for today, but I can come tomorrow. Maybe Seth and Joe could too, and I'll bring the post auger." Awesome. I forgot Kody had one of those. It'd been eons since one of us had anything new to erect.

"Sounds like a plan, I think I've got all the supplies we need. Even if we come up short, one of us could always run into the Lumber Depot in town." A quick call to Sam, the manager there, and he'd have whatever we needed ready and waiting.

"Sounds good. I'll see you bright and early tomorrow morning."

"Thanks Kody, see you then."

The vision I encountered when I walked inside, a dancing Twinkle, was a perfect addition to a perfect day. Tina jogged circles around him as he swayed his hips to the Christmas tunes he loved. I didn't want to be the bad guy, but I'd had enough of them and changed the station.

"Hey, how am I supposed to dance to this?" Twinkle protested, hands on his hips and with the attitude to match.

"Is that what you call all that hopping around?" I danced over to him, took his hand in mine and spun him around. The familiar giggles that warmed my heart filled the air. "Now this is called dancing, sweetheart."

Twinkle smiled and let me lead though I could sense he itched to throw in a twirly move or two. I wasn't the best dancer, but I could cut a rug without embarrassing myself. Around the room we went until the song came to an end. I took a bow and thanked my partner. "Thank you, kind sir, for indulging me in this lovely dance."

His smile lit up my world. "You are very welcome. Now, am I going to get in trouble if I put it back on Christmas tunes?"

"What do you think about leaving it here for a bit and share some of the music that I like. Maybe think of it as my turn."

Proper wording for the win.

His head bobbed up and down. "Okay, yes, taking turns. I can do that. That's fair."

"Mighty glad you see it that way," I winked, and he blushed. "Now, what are we filling our bellies with tonight?"

"Well, since I didn't know what the rest of the mystery meat in the freezer is, and you were kind enough to get some of what I liked today, I decided on baked fish with a salad and potatoes on the side." Twinkle was so proud of himself it was contagious.

"Well, that sounds mighty fine to me. Mind if I take a shower and clean off some of this sludge?" I glanced down at my clothes, covered in mud and who knew what else.

"Scrub away my handsome captor."

"Captor huh? I'm not sure how to take that. A captor usually means a person is being held against their will whereas you can come and go as you please." Twinkle covered his mouth to hide the giggles, which were still audible. "But I'll take the handsome part as a compliment, so thank you. Alright, silly goose, I'll be back in a few."

The song we had just danced to was stuck in my head and I caught myself humming it as I scrubbed myself clean. The outside air still had a chill, yet I broke a sweat while working. It would be worth it in the end though, to keep Twinkle and Tina safe. I'd meant to hit more projects on my to-do list around here but had let sleep get the best of me. Funny how I hadn't had the urge to nap much as of late. Was it possible that bad habit had been broken by the sweet little elf that came into my life?

My brothers showed up together bright and early the next morning. Basically, my family, excluding myself, lived in the same area of the mountain.

While Joe dove into digging the footers so we could set the poles, Seth mixed the quick dry concrete to cement them in place. Kody measured and cut the lumber while I got to work making a gate. My concept was a six-foot fence that we could see between the slats in case anyone or anything tried to sneak up on us. Tina shouldn't be able to jump over it but that's not saying certain wildlife couldn't sail over it and into the yard from time to time. We'd definitely have to keep an eye out for that, but the gate would be locked to help avoid any potential accidental escapes.

Twinkle brought out a huge plate of sandwiches for lunch and not long after we ate we called it a day. Between the four of us tomorrow, we'd have the project finished pretty quickly considering the hard part was done today. Joe was the burley buff one of the brothers and having him dig into that hard ass ground was better than Kody, Seth, or myself taking that task on. We'd have screamed and made-up new cuss words as we attempted to battle the semi-hard ground. To Joe, it was nothing. Hell, I'd seen that boy carry his two kids plus one of Jolie's at the same time. And trust me, his kids were just as strapping as he was.

"Monty, is everybody in town a bear shifter?" Twinkle asked as we settled in on the couch after dinner. Filled to the brim with shrimp and pasta equaled time to relax.

"No, sweetheart. There are a lot of humans in town. A couple know about us though not many do. This is LeClaire land, and we are the family that homesteaded here many centuries ago. While we're all bear shifters, not everybody around is. That fellow you saw me talking to when you were petting the horse at the shelter."

"Yeah, I got the impression you don't like him."

"Not one bit. He comes from a family of mountain lion shifters. They live on the opposite side of town. Let's just say he and I went a couple rounds in high school. For the most part they stay in their territory, and we stay in ours, but the town is to remain neutral. If any shifters are caught doing unsavory deeds there they're dealt with by their elder councils. And trust me, they don't want that because it can, and I've seen it happen, result in exile. To me, death would be easier than exile. Being shunned by your own was never a good thing."

Twinkle sighed and I feared I'd overstepped given the fact that he was shunned. "I'm sorry, sweetheart, I didn't mean to hurt your feelings. Come here." I patted my lap and he curled right up on it, just where I wanted him. I hated to admit it to myself, but I was falling hard for him. "Twinkle, what do think about going out on an actual date? I know we're mates and all that, but every couple I know dated first. We're kind of doing this whole thing backwards."

"Like a real date-date, like a dinner and movie date? The kind of stuff we've been watching in the movies that have the leg popping, swoony kisses?" Hope. That was what I read in his eyes and in his words. If knock your socks off kisses was what he wanted then damn it, that was what he'd get. How had I missed this?

"Twinkle you are too adorable for words." I kissed the tip of his nose. "Yes, like a date-date."

"I think that would be awesome. I've never been on a date. I don't know why I said that because you already know that."

His nervous rambling made me grin.

"But because I've never been on a date, I don't know what to do or where to go so I'm gonna let you pick everything, Monty bear."

"Gonna let me, huh?"

His head bobbed up and down.

"Alright, cutie. Monty bear will take care of everything. We'll go tomorrow night so be ready to roll at five on the nose." I kissed his nose again for emphasis and he sighed. I was beginning to believe I wasn't the only one falling for his mate.

The next night at five sharp Twinkle met me at the front door. It was almost like I picked him up yet here we stood in our own home.

"You look handsome, Twinkle." He'd put on a nice pair of slacks and a shimmering blue button up shirt. He was having fun with his new wardrobe and I loved that.

He shifted up on his tip toes and kissed my cheek. "And so do you, my Monty bear."

His Monty bear, how true that was.

"Did you get Tina situated?" Nothing worse than having a great night only to come home to a disaster. Bored pups much like bored kids were never a good thing.

"Yes, I put everything within her reach that I thought she might destroy up high and shut all the bedroom and bathroom doors."

"Good boy." I took his hand in mine, "Shall we?"

He nodded, and I pulled out my gentleman's card and opened the doors for him. It was different dating someone that you were destined to be with I suppose general chitchat would be the theme, the usual *tell me about your family* and *what do you do for fun* discussions. I didn't want to make Twinkle sad by bringing up things that would make him think of the North Pole and what he lost. He never spoke of a family and maybe he didn't have one. That kind of question would only serve to sour the mood, and I'd already promised myself I wouldn't upset him again. Being me I was sure that was a promise I shouldn't have made but either way I'd do my best to control my tongue.

We nabbed a great parking space at Cliff's Steakhouse. I jogged around to the other side of the truck to open Twinkle's door for him just as he reached for the handle.

"Why, thank you, sir." He flirtingly batted his lashes. Maybe we should pull back on the romance movies. I wasn't so sure I was able to live up to the expectations they set for him.

"You are very welcome. Shall we?" He wound his arm through mine as we stepped inside. "Good evening, we have a reservation for LeClaire." I told the hostess as we stepped up to the stand.

"Please, follow me." We followed the hostess back to a table along an exterior wall with a great view of the mountainside. I'd never tire of seeing it. I wasn't one that got the urge to stretch my wings and go somewhere new or move to the big city. I was perfectly content right here in Kodiak, on the mountain and living the life I had. It suited me and I had hope it would do the same for Twinkle and any future children we might have.

"This place is fancy, Monty bear."

"Nothing's too fancy for you, Twinkle. Now I know you're not a big fan of meat, but they have plenty of seafood choices. Me personally, I like the surf and turf. A big old slab of beef with a healthy side of shrimp." Twinkles' face morphed into equal measures of disgust and yum.

"Good evening, sirs. My name is Jacob, and I will be your waiter this evening. Can I start you off with a drink from the bar?"

"Two iced teas, please, Jacob. And we're ready to order whenever you are."

"Excellent, what would you like sir?" We gave him our orders, and as soon as he walked away my attention returned to my sweet date.

"Twinkle, you've settled in nicely. You haven't asked for much and you're definitely not as snarky as you were when you first got here."

Twinkle got that naughty gleam in his eye. "Oh, I'm sure I'll always have a snarky side. But for some reason being with you has just been easy. I haven't had to prove myself nor have I had to apologize for making mistakes. No acting up to get attention, or to be noticed. If I'm being honest, it was frustrating in the beginning when you slept all the time. Now that we're on the same schedule, it's comfortable. I don't know if that makes any sense. It's the first time in my life I've felt like me, like I belong. Having my world turned upside down was a huge wake up call."

That was the most Twinkle had shared of his past with me. "I completely understand what you mean. You've heard my family tease me about how much I slept versus what the rest do which made me odd man out. You're right it is comfortable. Maybe a bit unconventional, but we've made it work for us, and I think we're doing alright, don't you?"

"Yes." Twinkle's answer might have been simple, but his smile was sincere.

Our food came out fast. Subtle flirting and general chit chat filled the air as we ate. This was nice though I was a bit disappointed in myself for not coming up with the idea sooner. I paid the bill and just before we left, the owner, Cliff, caught us.

"Hey, Monty. Hey, Twinkle."

"How do you know my name?" Twinkle asked.

I slid my arm around his waist and kissed the top of his head. "Small town, sweetheart, everybody knows everybody and you're new blood and I'm sure Momma and her gossip chain got word around day one. Better get used to it, you're a LeClaire now. How can we help you, Cliff?"

"I'm considering a restroom remodel this summer, and hoped you'd give me a bid for it."

I'd done work for Cliff before, both here at the restaurant as well as at his own private residence. It was a no-brainer that I'd give him a quote and likely get the work. "I'd be happy to. How about I come by on Monday and take measurements and go over finishes. Then I can get the bid to you by the end of next week. Would that work? Right now, I'm on a date with my partner."

"Oh shoot. Sorry to interrupt. That'll work perfectly. You two enjoy your evening and we'll touch base on Monday, Monty. I hope you two enjoyed your meal."

"We sure did, thanks Cliff. See you then." When we got to the theater, as soon as we stepped inside Twinkle's eyes widened as he took in the décor.

"Wow, this place is amazing."

"Not as amazing as you. Do you want popcorn or anything to snack on?"

"No thanks, I'm still full."

He circled the lobby and stopped at every cardboard movie display while I got us a soda to share, just in case. The theater was nearly empty and since we had our pick of the seats we chose two in the center of the back row. As soon as the movie came on, his eyes once again widened in wild amazement and his jaw dropped.

"That's the biggest screen I've ever seen."

"Have you never been to a movie theater before, Twinkle?" It amazed me how many things I viewed as normal that were new to him.

"No, only watched them on TV. If this is what everybody does on dates, I approve."

"You are adorable, Twinkle. Movies often play a role in dates but there are many things you can consider for them besides this. When I was a teenager," I slid my arm around his shoulder, "we did sexy stuff at the movies on our dates."

"What kind of sexy stuff?"

I pulled him against me, taking full advantage of the new recliner seating for two and pressed my lips to his and immediately deepened the kiss.

"I think I like your version of dates."

We made out off and on throughout the movie. If you asked me what we saw, I'd have to look at the ticket stub in order to answer. Things heated up, no petting but... No matter what anyone says, erections while wearing denim was not fun and at my age, neither was coming in a movie theater. Having our first date end buck naked in my bed while in my dreams was fantastic, but it wasn't the impression I wanted to give Twinkle for his first date.

As soon as we walked in the house, he grabbed Tina's leash and took her outside and after they were done he joined me on the couch. Immediately, we returned to making out as though we never missed a beat. While Twinkle's hands never roamed past my chest, I wished they would, someday, though I was content for now within his comfort zone.

But when he clutched onto my shirt, I relented. "Twinkle, honey what do you want?"

"What do you mean what do I want? I'm very much enjoying this."

I smiled at his silly response and stole a quick kiss. "I am too, sweetheart. I know I'm ready for more, but I refuse to push you or risk making you uncomfortable."

He cocked his head, unable to decipher the words.

"In my world what we're doing is called first base. Second base involves more touching, and third is touching below the belt." His eyes widened as he absorbed the metaphor. "Going all the way, making love, is considered a home run."

"Oh-oh," he stuttered. "I don't think I'm ready for that."

"That's not a problem at all, darling. If you only want to kiss tonight, I'm perfectly fine with that. If you want more, I'm good with that too. Just tell me what you want or tell me to stop. You hold all the cards here and we move at your pace."

Twinkle's nonchalant shifting was anything but that. The outline of his straining erection was clear as day. You could see he wasn't in the most comfortable position with it however it was tucked. "If you want some help with that, I'm more than willing to assist."

"Help? What do you mean?"

This sweet little virginal twink would be my undoing. Hell, he already was.

"Help as in relieving the tension in that sweet cock of yours."

His mouth formed an O, but no words emerged.

"The way I see it I can either take care of it for you or you can take care of it yourself. The choice is yours and just for the record, there are no right or wrong answers."

"How-how?" Again, with the adorably innocent stutter. "How exactly would you take care of it?"

"I'd give you two choices, either with my hands, just as you would." His face flushed red. "Or with my mouth." So what if my voice took on a husky tone. I'd been dying to get a taste of Twinkle, and this was the perfect chance.

"Oh. I. Um." He paused, "You choose."

That was a no-brainer for me. Since I already figured he knew what to do with his hands this was my opportunity to dazzle him with my oral skills. "Is it alright if I touch you?"

His head bobbed up and down and I unfasted his pants and slid them down his hips, just enough to welcome my prize with a proper greeting. With my gaze on his, I licked a stripe up the underside of his shaft, extracting a shivery moan.

"Oh my god." He gasped, so I did it again.

I gently swirled my tongue around the tip and dipped it into the slit. Twinkle's sweet elixir was an aphrodisiac to my tastebuds. Given all the candy he'd eaten I half expected it to be sweetly reminiscent of a candy cane or a gum drop. When he didn't protest or tell me to stop I slid my mouth down over the shaft and drew his cock to the back of my throat as he chanted my name.

"Monty, Monty, Monty."

Given the fact he was a virgin, this would be over far before my jaw would cramp. Up and down, I bobbed, trailing my tongue around the head then sliding back down. I cradled his balls and gently tugged as I sucked, his cock throbbed in my mouth as he neared the end. I slid my finger down along his taint and gave his hole a light tap. As soon as I did, Twinkle arched up and had I not been paying attention I would've chocked. He writhed and moaned through his release, and I proudly swallowed every last drop.

Twinkle melded into the couch as though it swallowed him.

"Now that, sweetheart, is called a blow job and I hope you enjoyed it."

"Holy gumdrops! That was the most fantastic thing ever. It was like getting everything for Christmas that was on your wish list all at once."

That far too wholesome boy with his word choices. He made everything worthwhile. Even a sore jaw.

"I had a wonderful date Twinkle, but I believe it's time to tuck you in. Why don't you go put on your PJ's while I shut off the lights and lock up?" Were we safe out here? Absolutely, but I wouldn't put it past one of my family members to slip in and prank us via an unlocked door.

"Can I—can I—" He stopped and stared down.

I tilted his chin up and looked him in the eye. "Please don't ever be afraid to ask me anything, darling. Now, what were you going to say?"

He took a deep breath and let it out. "Can I sleep with you tonight?"

How in the hell would he expect me to keep my hands to myself? Well, fuck it.

"I've been waiting for you to ask me that." I stood and helped him up. "Let's go to bed."

Chapter Seven

TWINKIE

Springtime

"When do we get to plant the seeds?" I'd been staring at the growy seed things Monty called saplings for too long. We planted the seeds in tiny containers, and he kept them inside until they were ready to go in the ground. We'd gone to a plant nursery and picked them out along with a truck bed full of fruits and vegetables to plant a few weeks back. That was almost as fun as our dates had been.

Well, kinda the same.

But kinda not.

Ugh, my thoughts were all over the place as of late and I couldn't focus on one task for the life of me.

"Soon Twinkle."

Even Monty was getting frustrated with me, and I didn't blame him one bit.

"Come on, Tina. Let's go play."

The weather was perfect, and the snow long gone, which was odd to me given where I came from. Lush greenery from the surrounding forest flanked us on all sides. Wildflowers were in bloom and the bushes bore berries I couldn't wait to be ripe enough to pick. Flora and fauna at their finest. All these things I'd learned about I now got to experience firsthand, and I loved it.

"Maybe being outside was just what the day called for. Huh girl?" Tina barked and I scratched her head before I threw the ball again. She'd picked up the return part of fetching rather quickly and we had great fun playing the game now.

"We should have a picnic, let's see if Monty wants to join us." Tina was panting and ready for a nap after her workout. I brushed her off, she'd rolled in the grass and had all kinds of strange things in her fur.

She headed right for the water dish and barely made it to her bed before she fell onto it with a dramatic sigh. "Drama queen," I teased and rolled my eyes. "Monty, want to have a picnic today?"

He mumbled something unintelligible. "Ya, sure."

If he were any more enthusiastic I'd do a dance, just not to my favorite Christmas tunes. He put his foot down last week and forbade them. Grouchy bear.

I whipped up a few sandwiches, grabbed a blanket from the hall closet and set up lunch outside. Monty came out a few minutes later.

"Thank you, Twinkle. Sorry I've been so grouchy."

I didn't say a word. Just took a bite of my sandwich and kept my thoughts to myself. There were times when things were better left unsaid, and this was one of them. Guess I just met the new and improved Twinkle. Santa would be so proud of me. *Maybe...* There was no going back now to the old me that obviously nobody liked. Made me wonder if maybe Monty had started to feel the same way and had had enough of me. It was possible I'd worn out my welcome.

"What's that smell?" Monty sniffed the air, but I didn't smell anything outside of the surrounding plant life. Monty's head pivoted toward me, his pupils dialed, he snarled and ran inside the house. A few seconds later, I heard the front door slam and Monty's roar faded and he ran off. That was new. Not sure what had gotten into him, but maybe shifting and going for a run would wear the nasty out of him. I finished my lunch and enjoyed the peace and quiet with no negativity clouding the day. *Says he who was once the king of negativity.* Tina was still asleep, curled into a ball in her bed when I went back inside. I really wore her out this morning.

By the time Monty got back, the sun had set, and I'd already eaten dinner. Honestly, I didn't know what to say to him. I was angry and hurt he'd taken off and that I had to eat dinner alone. Evidently the feeling of how complete we were as mates was one sided.

Since I'd begun sharing a bed with him we would curl into each other, me tucked inside his arms, and he kept me nice and warm. I enjoyed falling asleep, twirling his chest hairs around my fingers. I thought we'd reached the plateau of consummating our relationship soon and becoming fully mated. Guess I'd given myself a false sense of hope.

By the time I got to bed after watching a new show I'd decided to binge, Monty was already fast asleep. I showered, stayed on my side of the bed, curled up with my stuffed Monty bear and cried myself to sleep. I was so upset but I knew tomorrow I'd have to address these issues with him. Hopefully it wouldn't result in us having our first fight though it kind of felt like we already were. What did I do so wrong that made him turn his back on me?

When I woke the next morning, Monty was already gone. No note, no nothing. Tina's dish had food in it, so at least he fed and took her out before he left. This was the first time I felt the need for a phone of my own. Up until now, Monty and I had done everything together, and I hadn't felt the urge to ask for one but now I knew differently. I had no one to call, no one to turn to.

Frustrated, I'd reached the end of my rope and things were changing one way or another. Staring at these containers of saplings on the counter had gone on long enough. They had to have been big enough to put in the ground and I wanted the space back for rolling cookie dough. We were running low, and I needed to bake some more. Making cookies always made me feel better. I only hoped it didn't fail me this time.

I slid into the rainboots Monty got me with little puppy paw prints on them and went out to the garden, pulled what I thought I'd need from the greenhouse and got to work. I had a plan in mind to keep the vegetables to one side and the fruits on the other. I was halfway through planting when I felt another's presence. Hoe in hand, I turned ready to clobber whoever was there only to find it was Monty.

"Is everything okay?"

The feral look on his face said anything but that and the fact he snarled at me was not a good sign.

"Um, your ears." He reached up and touched them, shocked to find they weren't human. His eyes were black, and he was clearly mid-shift. Unhinged was the best way to describe him and I was not at all comfortable with this.

"Should I be worried, Monty? What's going on?"

He moved forward and I took a step back.

"Monty, you're scaring me."

At this point, he had me pinned against the greenhouse and proceeded to sniff me like I was to be his next meal.

Monty shook his head and backed away. "I'm sorry Twinkle, I didn't mean to scare you. I'm just." He ran his hands through his hair and tugged. "I can't take this anymore. It's like I'm going insane, and the bear takes control."

My insides were on fire, my, well, you know, man bits were really awake. Like, painfully awake. His nearness increased the wet... Oh fizzle sticks. Ugh, I knew what that meant. I was in heat. I bet that was the scent he'd picked up on. Back at the North Pole we had pills they gave us to avoid this. I also lived alone there, so it was easier to ignore it and I wasn't compelled to go out and seek…Satisfaction, so to speak.

"I- I'm. sorry. I didn't mean to go into heat, but I don't have the pills anymore and I can't control it." Would he turn me away and reject me as his mate?

Monty snorted again. "Twinkle, you're all I think about, and I've scented you for days. I've done my best to control these urges. I've run countless miles, gone to my parents' house to wait it out but I couldn't stay away."

"You're avoiding me because I'm in heat?" I was on the verge of tears. He hated me.

"I'm avoiding you because you're in heat, which triggered my rut, and all I want to do is take you to the bedroom and take care of this. For both of us."

Gulp.

"Exactly. Given that this will be your first time, I can't guarantee I'll be gentle, and I hate that about myself. But right now, I have the urge to strip you naked and take you out here in the open where anyone could see us and that's not wise. I don't share what's mine and I don't put on shows for others."

Oh, so maybe he wasn't mad just…aroused.

Monty was right, consummating was part of our mating ritual, that much I did know. Now what else was involved he would have to fill me in later because I was fixated on this very important part. Like obsessively fixated to the point of rubbing on him to get off even though I knew that wouldn't be enough to satisfy the urge. Even so, I brazenly rubbed against him.

"I may not know much about mating rituals or bonding, but I do know this—there is only one way to take care of this. I just hope it's more than my being in heat that's attracted you to me."

"What do you mean?"

I shrugged. "We've been sleeping together for a while now and you've never tried to, you know."

"Twinkle, we were working at your pace, remember? Everything was up to you, I told you that from the beginning. Hell, I thought you weren't attracted to me. I didn't know it was the other way around." Monty kissed me. "Heat or no heat, Twinkle, I want you. Hell, I've already fallen in love with you. I was afraid of saying those words and scaring you off."

"Oh, Monty bear." The tears spilled over. Someone loved me, snarky faults and all. "I love you too. All this time I thought you hated me."

"No sweetheart. Hate is nowhere in my vocabulary when it comes to you. But right now, we have pressing matters to attend to. Bedroom matters. I'll be as gentle as I can but being this pent up makes it harder to control the feral side. There'll be plenty of time for love making later, I promise. But no matter how badly I want to be buried deep inside of you," those words forced a shiver. "This is as much your decision as it is mine. Are you one hundred percent sure you're ready for this?"

This intense fire inside me had to be extinguished, and Monty was the only one who could do it. The only one I'd ever let do it.

"I'm ready."

Monty threw me over his shoulder fireman style and speed walked inside. Guess that was the right answer. If this was his version of foreplay, I was more than good with that. Yes, I still watched far too many romance movies.

Monty locked the front door, muttering something about nosey families. When we got to the bedroom he sat me on the bed and tenderly caressed my cheek. Long gone was the wild animal who nearly attacked me outside, replaced by this gentle, handsome man who loved me.

"Sweetheart, do you want me to undress you, or do want to do it yourself?" He slid his shirt off over his head and I stared, mesmerized by the fact this perfect man was mine. My fingers already itched to trail across his chest, and lower. I trembled with need and urges like none I'd ever felt before.

"This has already taken too long." My pants were soaked. "And I can't believe I've said that considering *sex* is new to me."

He laughed as I whispered the word.

"But I'm more than ready so let's go."

Evidently that was the right thing to say. I was getting pretty good at not sticking my foot in my mouth. Monty had his clothes off and lay gloriously naked beside me before I so much as slid my rain boots off. Goddess, a naked Monty was an amazing sight.

"Twinkle, you're beautiful. Finally, I get to enjoy every inch of you."

"Yes, please."

I slid alongside Monty, and he took both our man parts in hand and stroked them together.

"Monty, I don't know about you but it won't take much. If you keep doing this, it's gonna be over too soon. All I can think about is…you know…" I was raised not to say bad words or that landed you on the naughty list. Even though I pretty much lived on it and my stocking was never filled with treats, I did still hang it by the chimney with care. If I would've cursed, Santa most likely would've taken that one perk away. It was bad enough I spent Christmas alone every year, but having the pretty holiday decorations that made me happy taken away would've been heartbreaking.

"I need to prep you first, Twinkle. Rough is one thing but hurting you is not an option." Monty reached behind me and ran his fingers down between my cheeks and slid two fingers inside. The intrusion may have been new, but it only served to ramp up my desire. I was feverish, unable to control these primal urges to be filled with Monty's cock.

"You're so wet, Twinkle."

I thought I was gonna die, the way his fingers moved inside me nearly drove me over the edge. This was heaven, and we hadn't even gotten to the good part yet.

"It's like you were made for me, Twinkle. Your body is perfect. Are you ready?"

"Yes." The word ghosted from my lips in a single breathless moan.

Monty positioned himself between my thighs and hovered above me. His intense gaze met mine as he lifted my legs and pressed his cock to my entrance. "Last chance to say no, sweetheart. Once I'm buried inside you there's no turning back."

"Please. Need you." I pleaded. The urge to be filled was like no other I'd ever had and it felt like I was coming out of my skin. I needed this on levels I couldn't fathom.

Monty easily slid inside, filling me in a single thrust. Once he was all the way in he bent and whispered in my ear. "Forever mine, Twinkle. I will love you and protect you until I take my last breath." His sweet words brought tears to my eyes for the second time today.

With every gasp and moan I released, he pushed harder, deeper, and thrust faster. His hips pistoned in and out until I could take no more and I screamed his name. "Monty!" as I came harder than I ever had. His knot swelled and he came with a wild roar. We lay there, sweaty, stuck together and I couldn't have cared less. That was by far the most amazing thing I'd ever done, cementing our bond as a couple should. Who knew heats could be this much fun?

"I hope it's not too uncomfortable for you, Twinkle. My knot, that is."

"No, Monty, it's perfect." He leaned down and kissed me. Dare I mention the bit about discomfort and a teeny bit of pain? No, Monty would likely pull out and insist on taking care of me and end it all and that I did not want to happen.

"It's a good thing, because we're stuck like this for at least another twenty or so minutes." He could move a bit but not much. Knotting at least gave us a break in between coupling. From what I understood, a heat could last up to three days and maybe it was the same for a rut. Hopefully one of us would be able to function long enough to take care of Tina. But right now, my body was ready for round two.

Monty stayed inside me while I shamelessly rode his cock through a second orgasm. By the time I was done, keeping my eyes open became a challenge. While I slept, he got up and took care of Tina and brought me a bottle of water. Alone I was somewhat fine, too tired to be bothered by mating urges but as soon as he crawled in bed beside me my body sprung to life.

"Sorry darlin', but this is gonna be hard and fast."

As far as was concerned, what we were doing was making love. The number of times he repeated how much he loved me and how beautiful I was and how happy he was to have me in his life as we cemented our bond was making love in my eyes. Those words were now permanently imprinted on my heart, which Monty owned.

I lost track of how many times I came over the next three days. Many wonderful firsts were had and beautiful memories were made. They say you never forget your first time and I planned to reflect on this until the end of time.

But what if I got pregnant?

Would Monty be upset or happy?

One way or another we'd know within the next couple of weeks.

"What are you thinking about so hard over there, Twinkle?" He curled up beside me, his fingers tracing figure eights on my stomach. We hadn't bothered with clothes. They'd have been nothing but a barrier to once again be removed. But now that our desires were finally sated, and we were able to catch our breath, I realized just how famished I was. We'd managed to nibble and drink our fill of water, but nothing that equated to a full meal. The way Monty tended to me, treating me like I was a porcelain doll, I loved it and ate up the attention.

"Many things we never discussed before, I guess. All of it just flooded my brain now that it's no longer laser focused."

Monty grinned. "Lasers are never a bad thing, but what had your brain spinning?"

"Well, family. Kids. Do you want any of your own? How many do you want? What if I'm pregnant?" I blurted out. I'd meant to breathe between words, but panic took over.

"Alright, slow down there, sweetheart. If you're pregnant, I will be thrilled. I've never thought about having kids before you but having a family with you would be wonderful. However many we have is whatever we have. You're the one who has to carry them for nine months so, you'll be the deciding factor on that."

Monty kissed me as I snuggled in beside him and drifted off to sleep. Nothing but warm, wonderful thoughts of what I hoped our future held. At least now I knew what had been wrong between us though, I wished he would have said something sooner to me. In the end, it turned out just fine. Better than fine, actually, and whichever way our life went we'd ride it out together the way it was meant to be.

Chapter Eight
Monty

"Good morning, sleepyhead." I greeted Twinkle with a kiss and a cup of hot chocolate as my tired mate wandered into the kitchen. I knew he was worn out after our three-day marathon and let him sleep in. He yawned and scratched his head. His hair stuck up in all directions which let me know he was still half asleep.

"Good morning." He took a sip of his drink. "Mmm, nothing better than hot chocolate first thing in the morning."

"Nothing, huh? I could think of a few things that beat that."

"Naughty bear."

"That's because I've got a sexy mate. Santa filled my stocking with the right toy." Twinkle nearly shot hot chocolate out of his nose. "You're not too sore are you, sweetheart?" I wonder what would be safe to use to help with any discomfort. Grace will know, I'll call her and ask.

"A little bit, but it was worth it. It's not too bad, I promise." Twinkle hissed as he took a seat.

"Not too bad huh? Your reaction says otherwise."

Twinkle blushed. "I put some lotion on it, but I promise I'm fine."

"You know, you can tell me anything, right?" That's the second time I'd had to say that and wondered how many more it would take before the words sunk in.

"Yes, and right back at you. I don't want it to get like it was again, Monty. If something's going on, we need to talk about it. I thought you hated me." Twinkle teared up and it took all I had not to drag him back to bed and remind him how much I loved him.

"My love, there's not a snowball's chance in hell I could ever hate you. I love you to the moon and back. I can't apologize enough for my actions. It was extremely difficult to be around you without ravishing every inch of your body. You deserve better treatment than that, especially for your first time." Though I wasn't quite sure I'd been successful in that regard. I recalled quite a few roars that escaped and the bed scooched across floor which reminded me, I better check and see if the floorboards were damaged.

Twinkle's giggle warmed my worried heart. "You properly ravished me, and I thank you for that." The little imp winked at me. "I do have a question though, are there any other aspects to this whole mating ritual that I should be aware of? Or was consummating it the only step?"

Jesus, Monty, did you ever speak to the poor guy beforehand? Way to break him into your world. Talk about failing miserably. "Not as far as mating goes. My brothers and sisters had weddings. That's more a human world thing but some want it. If that's something you want, we can definitely do it." Would he want a formal proposal?

"I would love that, further down the road. We don't need to rush into it when we already know we're mates."

"This is true, but I wouldn't mind putting a ring on it."

"And being the *it* in that statement, I wouldn't mind accepting your shiny new ring."

Decision made, now to get Momma involved. She would love this and would hopefully keep the secret to herself.

It was my turn to be the one with their mind going a million miles a minute. From finding the perfect ring for Twinkle, to watching that gorgeous man walk down the aisle toward me. Who would've ever thought this grouchy old bear would fall head over heels for a shiny Christmas star.

I whistled away as I whipped up a bowl of oatmeal for Twinkle and topped it with just enough cinnamon sugar that was the right amount for him but would've had the rest of us running laps to wear off the sugar high. I placed the bowl in front of him and took a seat and proceeded to shovel down a stacked plate of bacon and eggs. When was the last time I really ate? Considering how little we came up for air these last few days it was no wonder I was starving.

"Twinkle, I'm gonna run down and see Momma. Did you want to come with me?" As much as I loved taking him everywhere, I hoped he would say no, because I wanted to run my plan by her without him overhearing.

"As much as I love your mother, I kinda just want to hang out around here and relax and play with Tina if that's okay?'

"Of course, it is, sweetheart." I gave him a quick peck and grabbed the bag off the hook by the front door I used to hold my clothes in while I was shifted. It would sure feel good to stretch my bones after being in bed for as long as we had been. "I love you. I'll be back soon."

"Oh, that reminds me, maybe I should get a cell phone. When you took off the other morning and forgot to leave a note..." Twinkle side eyed me, and I got the point. "I got scared. It would be nice to be able to get a hold of you if I had to."

"By all means, I'm sorry I hadn't thought of that sooner. I'll take care of that for you while I'm out and about."

"Thank you. Love you too," he shouted over his shoulder as he dropped to the floor and rolled around with Tina. Those two were adorable. I stripped down, put the clothes in the bag, went outside and shifted and took off at a run toward my momma's house. I couldn't believe how excited I was about this, and the potential Twinkle could be with child.

Didn't take me long to get to my folk's house in this form. I'd never clocked myself to see how fast I ran as a bear, but I might consider it at some point. My brothers and I used to race one another when we were younger. Should've had dad time us then so I had something to compare.

I shifted just outside their house and dressed before I walked inside. Their door was always unlocked and us kids had a come any time open invitation. We were all raised here, my brothers, sisters, and I, and Momma said it would remain our home for as long as she lived there.

"Mmm, not sure what you're baking but it smells wonderful."

"To what do I owe the pleasure of our oldest son's visit?"

Dad was perched in his usual spot, the recliner, flipping through the TV channels.

"Well, I wanted to run something by you."

"Would it have anything to do with the last three days of you and Twinkle holed up inside your house? I heard there was a lot of snarling and growling going on." One guess who told Dad that...Kody.

Like father like son, neither of them had a filter nor knowledge of what personal space meant.

"Not gonna talk about what I do with my mate behind closed doors, old man."

"Don't you old man me. I can still take you."

I rolled my eyes and made sure he saw. "Dream on, old man."

"You two stop it," Momma called out. "Here, take a seat and have a piece of cake and tell me what's on your mind, Monty."

"Twinkle and I were talking about stuff. Come to find out he'd like to get married someday." Mom swooned. The woman loved weddings.

"So, I wondered what you would think about helping me pick out a ring so I can propose, properly."

The woman screamed so loud I had to hold my ears.

"I'd like to keep my hearing if you don't mind."

"Oh, hush you. Yes, I absolutely will, and I've got the perfect jeweler for you to use in town." She rambled off things about jewelry I had no clue about then dove right into wedding plans.

"Some of those decisions Twinkle has to make, Momma. Now the ring and the proposal, those are up to me. Just to set this record straight, if he's pregnant he may want the wedding to wait until after he has the baby."

"Oh my God. Oh my God." Momma squealed and jumped up and down. "That will be wonderful. You two will make the most beautiful babies. I can see them already."

"All right woman, calm down. He just came out of heat yesterday. But that's what I was trying to say, if he is pregnant, he may want to wait until after the baby comes. For now, I just need to find a ring. And get him a phone. Escaped my mind until he just pointed it out." Couldn't believe I hadn't already purchased one. "Do you have time to go into town with me today?"

"Absolutely." She took off the apron she'd had for as long as I could remember and hung it on the hook. "Let me get my handbag."

"What about me?" Dad called out from his resting place.

"What about you? You hate shopping." He'd reminded us of that every chance he got.

"No truer words have been spoken, son. I shall stay behind and hold down the fort."

I shook my head at him. I was truly blessed with the wonderful family that I had. But sometimes...

Mom chattered away all the way into town. From my place it was a half hour to an hour, given the weather, but from my folks and siblings places further down the mountains it was only about fifteen minutes. She went on and on about diamonds this, and sapphire's that then moved onto what about rubies? I knew the color for each of the stones, but picking a setting or a style I was clueless about. My hope was when the right ring appeared, I'd know. Or something along those lines.

We stopped at the phone store first, given that was the easiest chore. I opted for the same model I had for Twinkle.

It'd be easier to show him how to operate it. Had it added to my account and off we went.

"John Bovier. He's one of two jewelers in town. Your brothers got their wives rings from him as did your sister's husbands."

"Oh yeah, how did they manage to do that?" As if I didn't already know the answer given I was currently doing the same.

Momma smiled wide. "Everybody knows you come to the Momma first. If you don't, then there's probably gonna be hell to pay later. Happy Mother, happy boys." Woman made up her own metaphors that always centered around her. Go figure.

"Ha-ha. Ain't that the truth, Momma." Arguing was futile cause the damn woman was always right. Nobody crossed Momma.

We pulled in and parked and the man behind the counter's eyes lit up as soon as he saw Momma get out of the car.

"Sandy LeClaire," he met us at the door. "You're a sight for sore eyes. How are you doing?" He gave Momma a big hug.

"I'm doing just fine. I brought you the last of my children to finally say I do and pick out a ring for his beautiful fiancé to be. This is my oldest, Monty. Boy sure did take his time finding Mr. Right."

Mr. Bouvier threw his head back and laughed. "When the time is right, the time is right, and marriage isn't something to be rushed into. It's a pleasure to meet you, Monty," he said as we shook hands. "Now tell me a bit about your man."

"Well, he's snarky and sassy. Full of life and the happiest little man. Obsessed with Christmas." That was putting it mildly. "All I know is since he walked into my life, everything's been turned upside down in the best of ways."

"Now that is what we like to hear. Congratulations to you and your prospective fiancé. Now, what are you thinking? White gold, yellow gold, titanium. What's your metal of choice?" Mr. Bouvier rattled off.

When I glanced at Momma her face morphed into a giant shit eating grin.

"Well, to be honest, it's all Greek to me, and I don't know about jewelry. So, I guess just show us the metals you mentioned and when the right one pops out, either Momma or I will shout it out." Was that the right answer? Was there a right or wrong answer for this? Twinkle was grateful for the simplest of things, I was sure he'd be head over heels with whatever I gave him. Now clothes, that was something I'll *never* attempt to pick out for him.

Mr. Bouvier slid out a tray of each metal he'd mentioned from a locked cabinet.

"I think I like the white gold the best." Metal down, stones next. "What do you think, Momma?"

"Agreed."

"Great, step one is complete." He put the other two trays away. "Now, precious gemstones and design. Were you considering a simple band? Perhaps one with an engraved design, or were you thinking of adding stones?"

"Now you sound like Momma. I think she went through every stone known to man in the car ride here. I'm envisioning stones all the way around the band, diamonds possibly. Maybe throw in a couple sapphires. That is, after all, my favorite color now."

"Who knew my oldest would be the biggest sap? Yes, your Twinkle does have the most beautiful sapphire blue eyes I've ever seen. But then again, I've always been partial to brown."

Of course she was. My father had a unique shade of brown eyes whereas the rest of ours were nearly black.

"I don't know his ring size. Will that be a problem?" No clue how to get it without blowing my cover.

"No. If it needs to be resized that's not an issue. It's included with the purchase for as long as you own the ring." Mr. Bouvier was a straight shooter, and I appreciated that.

"Good to know. Momma, do you have any suggestions?"

"Well, I have an idea. I don't know if it's possible to do it, but if anybody can, Mr. Bouvier would be the one." She'd piqued my interest, and I was excited to hear it.

"What were you thinking, Sandy?"

"Would it be possible, and keep in mind, Twinkle is a little obsessed with Christmas." I'm glad she didn't go into the details as to why or we'd definitely lose our sanity card when she mentioned Santa. "It's his favorite time of year. What about integrating something holiday related into the design? Like little diamond and sapphire chips around the band that form snowflakes."

"Snowflakes, huh?" Mr. Bouvier sat back, deep in thought. As an artist I was sure he not only visualized the design but the craftsmanship it would take to bring it to life. "The band would have to be a bit wider, like this." He pulled one out that matched the width he had in mind. "I think I can pull that off and you know I'm always up for a challenge. Will be a beautiful one-of-a-kind piece."

"I couldn't think of a more perfect ring myself. That's genius, Momma." Was it normal to be this excited over a piece of jewelry? Where is Monty and what have you done with him, Cupid?

"You act like that surprised you. You know, I'm the smartest person in the family."

"And the humblest. How long will it take to make, Mr. Bouvier?"

"Honestly, not too long. I don't have any other custom pieces ahead of you. Why don't you give me about two weeks? If you haven't heard from me by then, give me a call back." He retrieved one of his cards off the rack and slid it in front of me. "If I complete it before then, I'll call you."

We agreed on a price, and I filled out the required paperwork with my phone number on it and paid the deposit. I had a vision in my head of what it might look like, and I couldn't wait to see the finished product. Twinkle would absolutely love it. Now, I just had to figure out the proposal.

Momma and I ran by the store so she could pick up a few things. I grabbed steaks and fresh salmon to grill so Twinkle wouldn't have to worry about cooking tonight. I wore the poor guy out though neither of had any complaints about it.

"Any ideas on the proposal?"

"No and I've got butterflies the size of Texas. No clue how I'll be able to keep this a secret."

And here I was worried Momma would spill the beans.

"Just wait until you've got the ring. Don't spill without the prize."

"Witty woman."

Chapter Nine

Twinkle

"Dance with me, Tina."

She hopped up and I held her front paws as we danced around the kitchen. Well, as best as she could on her hind legs. Monty was out working in the garden, and I was baking cookies. Hey, don't shame, they're my favorite treat and fast became one of Monty's too. We ate so many I had to replenish them weekly. I didn't mind because I'd found a dog friendly recipe online, so Tina got cookies too. I turned the music up as loud as I wanted and danced around and acted silly. Like a weekly date with the oven that ended with sugary yumminess.

Monty immediately changed the music as he stepped inside. We'd come to an agreement, a nonverbal one, that when he was around we listened to anything other than Christmas tunes. Some of his stuff wasn't too bad. It was kind of growing on me. He wasn't mean or nasty about it, but I understood. It was all I heard growing up and had no clue there was other music out there until recently.

"What would you like for dinner tonight, Monty?"

He snagged a cookie. "Surprise me, Twinkle."

Probably time to eat up some of what was in the freezer. Since I wasn't a fan of mystery meat, I'd leave those for Monty, but I deemed it leftovers night. I set one container out for Monty and decided to reheat the pasta with fresh vegetables I made from our garden yesterday for myself.

Multiple scents filled the air though the meat overpowered it all.

"Hey Monty, come and smell yours and tell me if it seems alright to you. I don't know what it is, so I have no clue, but it doesn't smell right to me." My stomach was doing loopy-loops, and this scent was the trigger.

He came up behind me, wrapped his arms around my waist and leaned over the saucepan. "Smells mighty fine to me, Twinkle."

I sniffed it again and my stomach lurched. I pushed Monty back and took off down the hallway and barely made it to the toilet in time. Everything I'd eaten for the extent of my existence came rushing out of me. This scared the *you know what* out of me, having never been sick before.

"Twinkle, honey, are you okay?" Monty grabbed a rag and wet it, then wiped my sweaty forehead.

"I don't know. That meat just didn't smell right to me." No sooner had I thought about it then all the cookies in the world came out.

"Let me get you some water. Stay put. Don't move." Monty returned a couple seconds later with a bottle of water and handed it to me. "Drink it slowly. Otherwise, it's gonna come blasting out of you too. I hope you're not getting sick."

"Me too. I have never been sick before. Everything was fine this morning. I had breakfast, no problem. I only snacked a little bit at lunch. Maybe I ate too many cookies." That was entirely possible.

Once there was nothing left in me, Monty picked me up and carried me to bed.

"Oh no," I popped up and immediately wished I hadn't. "What about dinner? Is it burned?"

"Sweetheart, it's under control. I already turned the burners off. Sit back, I'll bring you some crackers."

As soon as I was situated in bed, Monty ran back to the kitchen. Literally. Like he was afraid to leave me alone.

Figuring he wasn't letting me out of this room, I took the remote and flipped through the channels, prepared to settle in for the long night.

"All right, here are some crackers and a lime soda. These will help calm your stomach. Not sure why, but it almost always works. Tina is eating so I'll take her out in a few minutes. You doing okay?" He fluffed up the pillows and pressed the back of his hand to my forehead. "You're not hot which is a good sign."

"I feel better just tired. Who knew vomiting would wear you out?" Not me considering I'd never done it.

"How have you never been sick?"

I shrugged. "Santa's magic possibly? It was rare for anyone at the North Pole to get sick. Unless..."

"Unless what?" It took Monty a moment. "I'm calling Grace."

He bolted from the room and down the hall only to return a couple seconds later when he realized his phone was on the bedside charger. "Forgot my phone."

Why he didn't call her from here I'd never know, but he was out of sorts. Seconds later I heard the back door open, so he must've taken Tina out too. Not like running out there after him would do either of us any good and I was quite comfy. The crackers were bland, but not upsetting my stomach and there was no reason to test that by getting up.

Midway through the show, Monty came back in. Tina hopped up on the bed and curled up at my feet and I gave her head a scratch. "Daddy's good girl, aren't you."

"So, um," Monty paused, "Grace is gonna come by tomorrow and give you a checkup. I don't know what that entails but I'll be right here with you."

"I thought you had to start the renovation job on the restrooms at the restaurant?" I'd learned a lot over these last couple months like your bills aren't automatically paid here. You must have money for literally everything and the only way to get it is to have a job. Monty was the only one of us working and doing that. I felt useless but he said what I took care of at home was work enough and he was happy but if I decided I wanted to get a job he'd support that decision as well.

Now, if I was pregnant I got the feeling he wouldn't let me do much of anything. I think that made me what I heard on a silly housewife show something called a pillow princess.

I think...

Might need to research that a bit more.

"I called Cliff, told him I'd be a bit late. I'll head into town after Grace is done. You doing all right still?" How many times over the next nine months would he ask me that? I should make a game of it.

"What're you giggling about?" He gave me a sloppy kiss that only made me laugh harder.

"Nothing."

"You're a terrible liar."

Monty showered while I finished watching my show. When he came out he snagged the remote and set the timer on the TV. I'd gotten into a bad habit of falling asleep with it on. As soon as he was situated, I turned and curled into him. Normally, he'd pull me against his chest, but he hadn't tonight.

"Sorry, sweetheart. I wasn't sure you wanted to cuddle with your tummy on the fritz."

"I always want to cuddle. Are you going to treat me like a porcelain doll for the next nine months? If I'm pregnant, that is."

"Sure am." He kissed the top of my head. "You and that little LeClaire you're baking inside your oven."

"Great, now I'm a kitchen appliance. Plus, we don't know for sure that I'm pregnant." I didn't want to jinx it by admitting it aloud, but there was a tiny voice that whispered to me saying I was. Whether that was all in my head, who knew? What was more surprising was the lack of shock I felt at the potential of being with child. Maybe I was just ready for more and having a baby would cover that and then some. I'd envisioned a little one with Monty's handsome features, on the floor, playing with their toys. Giggling away when Tina licked their face. She would have so much fun with a baby.

"I read online that herding dogs are good for babies too. Stories of their heroic efforts when it came to keeping children safe were all over the internet. Tina would be a great protector and furry big sister."

"You are correct, my love. They are excellent at helping herd little ones. But you know me, I'll have every security measure imaginable in place. That reminds me, Tina's got her play area outside and I want to add onto it and install playground equipment for our offspring. Though that might attract the rest of the LeClaire youngins. Are we ready for that crowd?"

"I think so. I mean, we won't know for sure until our baby is here. I never really had a family of my own and I love yours. The elves preached they were family though they never included me in their merriment. I think they were just jealous."

"I think so too, my gorgeous mate." Monty snuggled me tighter and the one thought that came to mind was...

Home.

"I'm not sure what my parents did or who they were, because much like me they had been ostracized and never spoken of again. One of the older elves who had no family was asked to raise me. He was all about work and making his Santa happy. I was fed and clothed, we all were, it was a perk of being an elf, but I sought more attention and acted out in the form of making mischief. And here I am." Add another unsuspecting soul who unknowingly got stuck with me. Twice rejected, once accepted. Monty was my family now.

"Are you sad about that?" The doubt in Monty's words nearly broke me.

"No, I'm not. At first I thought you were for sure considering you were stuck with someone you hadn't chosen. But the more you growled the more determined I became to make you like me, although I know I went about it the wrong way. I'm not the brightest elf on the shelf."

Monty laughed, "Figure that one out, did ya?"

"Yes, humans have strange obsessions. Says he who is now one of them. Anyhow, changing everything in your home and your life wasn't the correct approach. Then when Santa told us in the letter that we were mated, I don't know, suddenly I wasn't sad anymore. The only downfall was that I was forced upon you with no warning. But I guess in the end, it worked out. I don't know if that makes any sense to you?" A rambling Twinkle wasn't always a good thing.

"It makes all the sense in the world, and you saw what my life was like before you came. I likely would have lived like a hermit until I died, much like that elf that raised you. He lived alone and now he'll likely die alone and that to me is a mistake. Honestly, it's a sad existence and I believe I was waiting for you all along."

"I like that theory. We're together now and that's what matters most. I'm truly happy, an emotion I never thought I'd experience. Nor did I ever imagine being mated let alone pregnant." That was putting it mildly. Never once in my life had I envisioned myself with child.

Monty chuckled. "Hopefully we'll find out tomorrow we've started a family."

I could hear the pitter patter of tiny footsteps as they ran across the wood floors, with Tina hot on their tail. Me in the kitchen baking cookies, of course. I didn't regret my life, neither the good nor bad experiences, because they led me to where I was now. Although being introduced to cooking shows might not have been the best thing. Poor Monty had been sent on quests for specialty items for recipes I wanted to test only to find out the local store didn't carry them. The manager said they'd be happy to order it for us, but I didn't want to be a burden.

Snuggled and warm, I drifted right off. My dreams, normally filled with all things Christmas, tonight instead were about babies. The what-ifs and unknowns of pregnancy and childbirth were almost too much to handle. Hopefully I wouldn't drive Grace mad with all my questions over the next nine months. If I were indeed pregnant. But if I was, then the baby would be born at the perfect time of year, December. Our first Christmas as a couple and our first as a family. Nothing could be more perfect.

"Knock-knock." Grace called out as she stepped inside with a bag in hand. "How are you two doing this morning?"

"So far, so good though if it's anything like yesterday, ask me again this afternoon and you'll likely get a different answer." Morning sickness was not fun and even less so at dinner time.

"Well, I've got a test for you to take that's going to tell us what we need to know. And if it's positive we'll listen for the heartbeat." Grace reached into her bag and pulled out a white box and handed it to me. "The directions are inside, but basically you pee on the stick that's in there."

"Oh, my." Why did I find that terrifying, yet being pregnant wasn't?

Grace smiled. "It's not as bad as you think. Go do your thing and then we'll wait a few minutes and see if it gives you a smiley face or not. For humans, they usually have to wait a few more weeks before they can take a test. But for us we can find out within a couple of days after a heat. Not sure if it's a gift or a curse. Which may be why Aiden and I stopped at one."

Grace, and her husband, Aiden, only had Kaleb. He was sweet as pie with his little chubby cheeks but just entered what they called his terrible twos. No clue what that was exactly but I foresaw numerous internet related searches in my future. I definitely wasn't taught anything about children other than what they wanted for Christmas. I saw them around town but never babysat or interacted with them, so this was one-hundred percent new territory for me.

I shut the door behind me and sighed as I pulled the directions out and read them. The process was as simple as Grace mentioned. I peed where I was supposed to, which I would have to say was the most uncomfortable part of all of this, because it was weird. I sat on the toilet while I waited and listened to Monty's heavy footsteps as he paced the hall. At one point, Grace told him to sit down but he growled at her. All bark and no bite, that was my sweet bear. If it came down to it, I knew without a doubt he'd defend me if he had to, though I hoped the need never arose.

"Um, Grace," I called out.

She knocked on the door. "Can I come in?"

"Yeah, I um, I think you better."

She stepped inside and glanced at the stick on the countertop. "Wow, that's fast. You've only been in here like two minutes."

"I guess we have our answer." I glanced up at Monty who had walked in behind her. He looked at the stick, then at me, and scooped me up and swung me around.

"This bathroom is not big enough for that, brother but congratulations are in order. To Daddy and Papa or Papa and Dada or whatever you two determine you want this baby to call you. I couldn't be happier for you." Grace hugged us both. "Alright, Twinkle, why don't you go lie down and I'll be right in. I want to do a quick exam and listen to your belly and see if I can hear the heartbeat."

I skipped down the hall, jumped on the bed and landed with a bounce, then realized I probably shouldn't have done that. I'd guess there will be a lot of things I'd have to stop or slow down on over the coming months. I hoped Monty wouldn't have to roll me through the house like the blueberry girl in that movie we watched the other night. Can they juice a pregnant omega?

Grace blew on the end of the silver thing she pulled from her bag and when she caught my curious eye she realized I had no clue what was happening. "This is the stethoscope. It helps me hear the baby. This round metal piece gets cold, so I blew on it to warm it up. Didn't want it to shock you."

"Much appreciated. Thank you."

She slid it around on my belly until she found the spot and grinned up at me. "Would you like to hear, Twinkle? It's your baby's heartbeat."

"Yes please, yes please, yes please," I merrily chanted, beyond excited to hear it. She put the earpieces into my ears and there it was, the faintest little *thump, thump. Thump, thump*. "Monty, come listen."

He came around, and I slid them into his ears. As soon as he heard it his face lit up like a Christmas tree. "We did it Twinkle. We have a baby in there!"

"You two have done well, the heartbeat is strong. Twinkle, I'll keep an eye on you and will come by for regular visits. I'm the midwife for the pack, in case my brother forgot to explain that. That means I'll be the one to deliver your baby which brings me to confidentiality. Family or not, you are now my patient, and I promise you privacy. The family will only know what you and Monty tell them, nothing will come from me. Understood?"

"Yes and thank you. I think it would be fun for Monty and I to be the ones that tell them."

"It's your story, your life and no one has the right to take those important moments from you. When it's time for the baby to be born, you can either have it in bed or in the bathtub. Some have credited the relaxing water for an easier delivery—either way that's up to you. Whomever you want with you and Monty during the delivery is up to you as well. Labor is a private matter though some like their entire families present for the birth. I am not one of those people, but I did have Momma and Aiden there with me. Momma actually delivered Kaleb because Aiden nearly passed out."

"Oh my Goddess," Monty laughed. "I hadn't heard about that."

"Yes, and I'd wisely ask you to forget it. I lost a lot of blood and had to be stitched up."

That did not sound fun. "I can't imagine everybody seeing my bits. Well, assuming it's my bits that will be bared. Wait, where does the baby come out of?" My god, how had I never thought of that before? There was no way it would come out of that little hole on the end of my...

"Deep breath, Twinkle." Grace ran a soothing hand up and down my arm. "Your Omega body was built for this. The baby will be born rectally for you as a male."

I must have stopped breathing because she patted my chest and reiterated the need to breathe. "Twinkle, you're breathing for two now. Your channel and anus will dilate to the size it needs to in order to allow the baby to pass through. It's not as bad as it sounds. I can send you the links to videos to watch if you'd like. There are also birthing classes I offer that would be perfect for you."

My head went side to side so fast I nearly vomited. "No, please don't do that. I don't think I'd enjoy that, and it may scare me more. Blood and all that."

"He can't handle it in movies either," Monty chimed in.

"Not a problem, I won't send them but if you change your mind on the birthing classes let me know. You have my phone number and Momma's too. She adores you and will help however you need her to. You can text me anytime, and you can call me as long as it's not late except in the case of an emergency. You'll soon find out what it's like to have a two-year-old, and you'll be thankful for any sleep you can get. I'll be over once a month to check on you for the first two trimesters, for the third it will be bi-weekly until we near the end then it will be weekly unless I feel otherwise. Fair warning, once you tell the family you're gonna have a lot of LeClaire's in your business offering advice you didn't solicit."

"I thought they already did." I hoped that was rude, it wasn't meant to be but I'd received advice from every LeClaire since day one.

"I'm sure they have. But now as the pregnant mate of the oldest LeClaire child, you'll be doted on and driven mad. Take it or leave it. Every pregnancy, childbirth, and baby are different. There are certain things that are good to know ahead of time, and other advice is worthless."

Chapter Ten
Monty

"I'm gonna be a dad!" I randomly announced to the restaurant as I stepped inside. No clue who was here, it just came tumbling out. The excitement of being a father couldn't be contained.

"Congratulations!" the hostess replied, as the nearby tables clapped and uttered their congrats.

"Thank you. Sorry." Lost in my own world and forgot the filter. "I'm Monty with LeClaire. I'm here to start the bathroom renovation today."

"Oh yes, let me get Cliff."

"Hey, my friend," Cliff said as he came into the lobby. "I understand congratulations are in order."

"Yes, yes, they are, and I couldn't be happier." That was putting it mildly. I was so damn excited I obviously couldn't contain it.

"Excellent. We've got the first restroom stanchioned off and ready for you. Signage is in place directing the patrons to use the other. If it gets a bit hairy and they complain we may consider a couple portable units be added to the parking lot."

"Well, let's play it by ear. If all goes well, I'll have the demo done today and will start the installations for the new flooring and fixtures tomorrow. I drove around back and saw they dropped off the dumpster so we're good to go." I loved it when a plan came together with no delays.

"Excellent. Well, you know where everything is and how to get a hold of me. We'll let you get to it." Cliff headed off toward the kitchen while I wandered down the hall to the restrooms.

I was surprised when he told me that I could demo while they were open, but I'd do my best to contain the noise. Hopefully, none of the plumbing lines would need replaced, because I didn't include that in the bid. Just made note that if I found anything that wasn't in the visual assessment we'd do a change order for the additional fees to complete it. As of right now, the plan was new floor to ceiling tile, new sinks and faucets, new toilets, new paper towel and toilet paper dispensers, and new stall dividers. The only area that would be painted was the ceiling. Not a fan of painting but I'd do it when requested, though this time I would delegate the job to Kody.

I got right to work, removing the stall dividers and whistling a happy tune. Didn't think to bring my iPod, my brain was obsessed with all things baby, and it skipped my mind. *Light bulb!* How had I not already thought of this? I felt terrible for cutting off Twinkle's Christmas tunes when I was home, but I'd reached the end with them. *So why hadn't my dumbass bought him his own iPod?* Then he could listen to them to his heart's content. I shook my head at my own blunder and made a mental note to stop by the electronics store on the way home and buy him one. Something shiny to match his fancy clothes. He was by far the best dressed person in all of Kodiak.

I knew, without a doubt I'd spoil the baby, and I lovingly did with Twinkle. I'd waited forever for not only a relationship I never knew I wanted, but a family of my own. I'd given up hope that my mate even existed. Then along came Twinkle and soon we'd be three. Holding my own daughter or son, gender was irrelevant as long as it was healthy. But once I held them, I'd be addicted.

"Whoa." I stopped to take a swig of water and glanced around. In my brain fog I managed to remove the stalls, toilets and sinks and took them to the dumpster. The brain was a scary thing for sure. Now all that was left was to remove the ancient linoleum flooring. I reached for the adhesive remover when in walked Cliff with a tray full of food.

"Lunchtime, Monty. Time to take a break." His eyes widened. "Wow, you've got a lot done."

"Got lost in the work and just kept going. Demo's my favorite part of any job. I consider it my own form of therapy."

Cliff laughed. "But if the rest of the job goes this smoothly, we should be out of your hair in four to five days and just in time for the weekend crowd to test it all out. Kody will be in tomorrow to paint the ceiling, Joe and Seth will help set the tile. The final day will be grouting. Then next morning I'll be in to clean and then you'll be good to go. We'll wait a week before we dive into the other one if that works for you."

"That works perfectly. Monty, you've never disappointed me with any of your work, and I was glad you were able to fit me into your schedule."

Schedule such a funny word because pre-Twinkle, I'd slept more than worked. Now that I wasn't being lazy, I'd be able to take on more jobs. Babies were expensive and I'd be damned if ours would ever go without cause its Papa was a lazy bear.

Welp looks like I've deemed myself Papa.

All those bid requests that went unanswered. If I didn't work, my brothers grabbed odd jobs when they'd rather we worked as a team on larger projects. No wonder they bugged the shit out of me. Clarity was an amazing gift. Hell, calling and scheduling bids was the perfect job for Twinkle. He'd been bored out of his mind and asking to help so this would work well for the family as a whole.

The fantastic steak sandwich Cliff whipped up was gone in three bites. Finished up and got to work on the flooring demo. The glue had failed in more spots than it remained adhered to and while it didn't come up in one piece, which would have been nice, it came up in several big ones. The adhesive remover was applied to the tough spots and in no time I had it scraped up and called it a day.

"Honey, I'm home." I hollered to Twinkle as I stepped inside the house, only he was nowhere to be found. Then I realized what time it was and ran straight for the bathroom and there sat my poor pregnant mate on the floor beside the toilet and white as a ghost.

"Oh, sweetheart, I'm so sorry. I meant to come home earlier, but I was in the zone and got the demo done." I sat beside him and rubbed his back. "I'm so sorry, honey. What can I do to help?"

"It's not your fault. Well, no, I guess it kind of is but not in a bad way." Poor guy lurched forward again.

"Let me go get you some water. I'll be right back."

I'll set an alarm on my watch to ensure going forward that I'd be home earlier than I was today until the morning sickness passed. My poor, tiny Twinkle didn't have much to donate to the porcelain God. I hated to see him like this. I loved my happy little shiny singing elf.

Much like last night, I got him situated in bed again with crackers and a lemon-lime soda, then showered and fed myself. When I returned here he had the TV turned to the same show he watched last night. The poor thing was exhausted. Tina was curled up beside him and he petted her in slow, soothing strokes, his eyes heavily-lidded as the repetitive motions calmed him and he zoned out.

As quietly as I could, I slid into bed and set the timer on the TV, figuring he forgot. Tina was between us, with his hand resting on her back but they were still close enough that my arm stretched across them both and I could somewhat hold Twinkle. My poor pregnant omega. I hated this part for him even though I was selfishly excited as I knew he was, too. And when he woke, I'd have a gift that would brighten his day.

"Good morning, my love." I rolled over and kissed Twinkle after I shut off the alarm.

"Morning. I already took Tina out and started your coffee," he yawned. "I've been up for a while."

"How are you feeling?"

"Better. I wish I didn't have the afternoon yuckies though," He made a disgusted face. "Not enjoying that part at all."

"I bet you're not. Let me get dressed and I'll meet you in the kitchen. I have a gift for you."

He hopped up and down on the bed. "A gift for me? Really?"

"Really." I kissed the tip of his nose and popped out of bed. "I'll meet you in the kitchen in five. I'll be the one with the flannel shirt. You can't miss me."

Twinkle laughed. "You're so silly. Isn't Monty silly, Tina?" She nuzzled his hand. Seeing Twinkle this happy filled me with a joy like no other.

"Look at that, cooking me breakfast. You spoil me, oh sweet mate of mine."

"Says he who takes care of me every night."

I pulled him into my arms and stared down at his handsome face. "I love you. Plus, it's my job."

He pouted. "I don't want to be your job."

"Okay then, it's a duty I do with pride and honor." He stared blankly up at me. "Cat got your tongue, Princess?"

"Brat. Besides," he swished his hips, "I believe you mentioned a present?"

"Right, thanks for reminding me." I crossed the room to my work bag and pulled the box out. "Here you go." He'd have no clue what it was, but the confusion was half the fun while watching him open it.

"What is it?"

"It's your own iPod. You put music on it and place these earbuds in your ears then you can listen to Christmas music year-round without my grouchy butt complaining and changing the radio station."

He turned it from side to side, peered at the bottom where the charger plugged in. "How do you get the music on it?"

"Well, there are instructions in the box but it's easiest if you do it from the laptop. Give it a try and if you can't figure it out I'll set it up for you tonight when I get home. Oh, that reminds me. Did you still want to help with reno jobs?"

"I do, very much but what about the not so fun afternoons?"

"That's why the tasks we need you for are perfect for you. This weekend we'll sit down, and I'll show you. Basically, you'll be calling potential clients back that my lazy ass ignored for sleep."

"You said a bad word."

"I did though I have gotten better about it." Just saved it all for when he wasn't around.

"Yes. I can do that. I'm excited, now I'll be contributing."

"Honey, you already are. You take care of the house and you're baking our little one, too. That's a lot."

"Hee-hee, baking."

"Have you given anymore thought to when you want to at least tell Momma, who you know will announce it to the world. Fair warning, that woman is a human megaphone."

"Sweet jujubes! I completely forgot. I've been floating in our humble bubble here though being sick has taken some of the fun away. Wait" Twinkle's arm shot up in the air as though he was commanding a crowd. "I have a fun idea. Why don't we start a group chat with your mom on our phones and text back and forth about a baby between you and me like she's not there. You and I both know she'll call a second later."

"That is brilliant. What did you have in mind?"

Twinkle grabbed his phone off the counter and fired off a text. My phone chimed and as soon as I saw what he wrote I lost it. This was perfect.

> *Twinkle: What color do you want to paint the room?*

> *Me: Something neutral since we don't know if it's a boy or a girl.*

Twinkle counted aloud. "One, two," then before he said three the phone rang, and I answered it on speaker.

"What baby? Whose baby?" Momma rapidly fired off. No hello or how are you, just straight to the point. "Who's pregnant?"

Had she already forgotten our discussion at the jeweler the other day or was she playing it up. I hadn't told Twinkle about that, so I had to play along, too.

"I am, Sandy." Twinkle grinned even though she couldn't see him.

I nearly dropped the phone when Momma screamed. "Oh. My. Goddess. I'm gonna be a Grandmother Levi. Levi, did you hear?"

Dad's friendly voice echoed in the background. "Yes, this whole side of the mountain just heard you woman and FYI, you're already a grandmother."

"When are you due? Do you know what you're having? Why am I just now hearing about this? Shouldn't I have been the first one you told?" Another expectation, the motherly guilt trip.

"Second, Momma. You know Grace was the first since she's the midwife. Twinkle's due date is the week of Christmas." How serendipitous was that? My sweet elf was having our baby during his favorite season.

"Oh, I believe it. Santa has a mysterious way of working, doesn't he?"

"I can pretty much promise Santa had nothing to do with this, Momma." The woman had lost her mind. As far as I knew, Santas had zero control when it came to heats and ruts. At least I hoped they didn't. I viewed that as a level of creepiness I didn't care to explore.

"We need to have a baby shower. We need to get that room done. Twinkle, you can't paint. You can't be anywhere near it or cat litter boxes." Stage two, barking orders. There was a method to the woman's madness, I thought...

"Momma, we don't have a cat." She truly tripped and sailed over the deep end.

"Twinkle, I'll take you into that baby store that's in town, and we can register you for all the things you'll need. Like baby furniture, clothes, diapers, a breast pump."

"Breast pump?" Twinkle asked, his face a myriad of confusion.

"Yes, I have so much to show you. Twinkle, I am so excited." That was putting it mildly. Momma rambled on and Twinkle appeared overwhelmed, so it was time to wrap this up.

"Momma, he's had awful morning sickness in the afternoon. Grace and I are keeping a watchful eye on him. You might want to wait before you attempt to take him out and about, just in case. At least let him get through this first trimester and see if the nausea dissipates."

'You poor thing. I've been working on new meatless recipes and soups for you. I'll bring some over later. But not too late, and some bread I baked. I need to check on my Twinkle."

Her Twinkle.

His face lit up like his beloved Christmas tree when she said that. Look at me with the holiday metaphors. Guess my sweet mate rubbed off on me. It was so important to him, being a part of a family, and I couldn't be more thankful that my pack were as open and accepting as they were. Many in the shifter community had same sex partners, it was second nature to us to accept everyone for who they were, unlike humans. One of many things I'll never understand about their kind.

"Okay, Momma, we've got to go. I have to work, but Twinkle will be here. Just do me a favor and text him first before you come up to make sure that he's not napping. He needs all the rest he can get." Protective mode engaged. If Twinkle thought I treated him like a porcelain doll before, he was in for a bubble wrapped surprise because if that's what it took to keep him and the baby safe, I'd invest in a factory full of it.

"Yes, yes, of course. I'll do my best not to overwhelm him."

In the background, my dad shouted out, "Lies, all lies. She's lying to you."

"Oh, that man." She fired back. "I'll deal with you when I get off the phone, Levi."

"And on that note, it's time for Twinkle and me to say goodbye. Love you, Momma." I couldn't disconnect the call fast enough.

"Monty bear, I'm overwhelmed. I didn't know about any of these things. How will I be a good daddy if I don't even know the first thing about babies?" That beautiful pouty lip made a heartbreaking appearance and shivered as he held back the tears.

"Sweetheart," I took Twinkle's hands in mine. "I'm barely a step ahead because of all the nieces and nephews I've got running around, but I've never changed a single diaper. We will learn together, I promise, and we've got enough family around to help us, not to mention free babysitters. It'll be fine, trust me, Plus, you know any questions that you have, Grace and Momma will answer and there is always your new best friend, Google." That brought back the smile I loved.

"I do enjoy that friend, it's been most helpful with questions I have in this new life of mine though some of the stuff that pops up is scary." Twinkle shivered.

I couldn't imagine what he saw.

"I'd advise you narrow your searches to exact words before you end up somewhere you really don't want to be. There are horrible things out there that will give you nightmares." His eyes widened. "Yes, be very specific in what you search for."

"Good to know and I promise to be more careful."

I kissed his forehead. "I know you will, my love," and finally pressed my lips to his. "I've got to run. Kody, Joe, and Seth are meeting me at the restaurant. It's tile laying day. I will do my best to be home before, well, you know." I dared not say the word *vomit* and curse this morning's good fortune.

"I do. Are there any pills I can take or anything I can do to make it stop?"

"I wish you could, sweetheart, unfortunately, that's all part of the baby making process. Plus, taking certain medications while pregnant can be dangerous to the baby. Don't try anything without first consulting Grace. Okay?"

"Okay," he wiggled his hips. "The making part was awesome but the baking part not so much."

"Twinkle, you're a poet and didn't know it. That had to be one of the best lines I've heard in a long time. I'll see you later, sweetheart. Love you."

"Love you too, Monty bear."

Chapter Eleven

TWINKLE

"Monty, what if I get so big I can't fit through the door?"

"Twinkle you are three-months pregnant, and you barely have a pooch."

I rubbed my belly, thinking of the tiny cookie baking in there. "I love my little pooch."

"I love your pooch too. How's the schedule coming for the team this week?"

"Not too bad. You have the Hanson house remodel that starts this week. As soon as that's done, you dive into the employee breakroom at the Bridal Shoppe. I've got Kody working another job right now."

I'd taken to this new role that Monty created for me within the company like a natural. I knew nothing about construction, but quickly learned faster than I'd absorbed anything from the pregnancy books I'd read. Somehow, administrative tasks just kind of clicked for me and the software that Monty used was packed full of useful information. Anytime I typed in the square footage and the job type, it populated with options for materials that fit. I'd select what we'd need, and it calculated the total for each item and completed the bid. Monty still double checked the proposals to ensure I hadn't missed anything but for the most part, he was pleased.

"Well, my brothers sure are happy to be back to work full time, including Aiden. I was such a jerk for ignoring their needs. They struggled because I was a lazy bear."

"Well, now it's come together nicely, and everybody seems to be happy." I'd even started watching some of the nieces and nephews here and there when Monty's siblings had to work. I guess the dads had stayed home and babysat while Monty slept and the mother's worked. It was fun and gave me hands on experience, and better prepared me for our upcoming addition.

"That reminds me Twinkle, Momma wants you to call her about the baby shower. Did you want me to meet you at the baby store to set up the registration for what we need? By the way, don't order a crib. Momma said she had dad pull our old one out of storage. Don't worry if it's not perfect, I can fix it up any way you want it."

"The very crib that baby Monty slept in. I'm so excited. Do you know which teeth marks on it are yours? I want to keep them. We can fill in everybody else's. I just want yours." How weird was that to say?

"I might be able to pick out a couple of them, but not many especially since it went through not only my siblings, but the nieces and nephews too. For a while there my parents kicked kids out like Tic-Tacs."

"I don't know what that means, but it doesn't sound fun."

"Well, they were having fun, and that was the problem. Then came along the Tic-Tacs meaning my brothers and sisters. There's barely a year between each of us birth wise."

About that time Aiden walked in with Kaleb. "Did you forget how to knock?" Monty said as he shook his head at him.

"Don't listen to him, you're family." I took Kaleb from Aiden and stuck my tongue out at Monty as I sat Kaleb on the floor in front of the bucket of toys we now had. I pulled out his favorite truck and handed it to him. "Kaleb is spending the day with Uncle Twinkle."

"Cookie," Kaleb said as he made grabby hands. Aiden shook his head.

"Yeah, he's turned into a cookie monster, and I think we have Uncle Twinkle to blame for that." Aiden's words held no malice, the grin on his face said as much.

"I can guarantee you have Twinkle to blame for that," Monty snagged a cookie himself. "But what's the fun of having nieces and nephews if you can't send them home all sugared up for their parents?"

Aiden did that thing with his middle finger Monty said meant a dirty word and I shook my finger at him.

"Little hands learn naughty gestures," I warned him.

"Naughty," Kaleb mimicked from the floor and even though they laughed that proved my point. The little pudgy monster was quick and adorable, and I enjoyed my time with him.

"Grace only has a couple of appointments this morning and said to tell you that she should be by to pick him up around lunchtime. From the sounds of it she planned to have lunch with you today, Twinkle."

"Sounds wonderful, Aiden." I only hoped it didn't come back up later or worse, while she was still here. When would this vomiting nightmare end?

Monty and Aiden left for work, and I put cartoons on for Kaleb and gave him a cookie to snack on. "Here you go, sweet boy."

"Cookie." He made grabby hands again. Tina sat nearby awaiting gifts in the form of crumbs. I hardly had to vacuum with her around.

Kaleb and I munched on our cookies and watched cartoons while playing with his building blocks. I'd stack them and he'd crash his toy truck into them and giggle. His laughter triggered mine and that was how Sandy found us, rolling around on the floor being goofballs.

"Knock-knock," Sandy said as she came inside. I'd learned to leave the door unlocked so the LeClaire brood could come and go as they pleased. Less of a hassle than getting up to answer the door fourteen times a day. Not that I minded, but this was just easier for all.

"Gamma!" Aidan wobbled over to her, and she scooped him right up.

"How is grandma's little bear today?"

"Cookie." He knew very few words but the ones he did know he utilized to their fullest.

"I promise he does know more than that word."

Sandy just shook her head. She knew me and my minor—not so minor obsession with the sugary confections.

"How are you feeling today, Twinkle?"

"Right now," I glanced at the new watch Monty got me that tied in with an app on our phones. He claimed it would alert him if something was wrong. I didn't see how, but if it made him feel better I'd wear it. "I'm okay, and I'm hoping it stays that way. I really wish this morning slash afternoon sickness would go away. Makes it very hard to enjoy having our little one inside me when all it's doing is making me sick." I rubbed my belly and whispered. "Daddy loves you, sweet one."

"Yes, I more than understand that. With Monty I was sick as a dog for the first six months. I kid you not."

"Six months? There will be nothing left of me by then." My heart raced and set me on the verge of an anxiety attack. Six months of vomiting every single afternoon. No, just no.

"Twinkle," Sandy rubbed my back. "Just breathe. It will be okay, I promise. Hopefully that won't happen to you."

Kaleb yawned and rubbed his eyes. I filled his sippy cup and held him until he fell asleep, then carefully laid him in the collapsible playpen to nap.

"See, you're a natural, Twinkle. You're going to make a wonderful Daddy."

I hoped for our little cookie's sake she was right.

"Now, if you're feeling up to it this weekend while Monty and the boys are working on the baby's room, we can take a trip into town? Have a nice lunch and stop by that baby store I mentioned."

"That actually sounds wonderful, plus it will be nice to get out of the house for a couple of hours. Not that I mind being home but it's just nice to stretch your wings, if you know what I mean." I wasn't sure I knew what I meant so how could I expect her to?

"I absolutely do. Have you read any of the books I brought you or visited the websites I sent you the links for?" Sandy had a wealth of knowledge and has done her best to calm my nerves.

"I've been out to all the websites, but I only finished two of the books. I don't know. Some of it's just icky." I scrunched up my face, recalling images I'd rather not have seen.

Sandy grinned. "Icky is probably the nicest way to put it. When it happened to me the words I used would have turned your face red. Do you understand the breastfeeding part now?"

When I nodded she visibly relaxed. Breast feeding was a huge part of this, and it was important I grasped it.

"So, we've knocked that worry off your list?"

"Yes, thank you for that. I'm good with nursing though I'm not sure about pumping it out. But if Monty wants to go out and do anything and you guys are watching the baby, I'd have to. I'm gaining a better understanding, especially with the expenses associated with having a child. I'm enjoying my new role within the family business. I'm a good helper."

"Yes you are, but you also must understand that in our society, and it was probably the same where you came from, though this part wasn't shared with you. Omegas tend to take care of the family and don't work outside of the home. Trust me, don't discount an omega's importance. Any alpha worth their weight will tell you that. But like Grace, she works, but her job is assisting the omegas in not only childbirth but in rearing children. Each family is different and how that family operates should only matter to the family operating it, if that makes sense to you. What and how you and Monty decide works for your family only matters to you and Monty and that's the way it should be. It's nobody else's business who works or doesn't or who does the cooking. If Monty decided he wanted to stay home and you went to work, that would be between you two. Trust me, taking care of a family and a house is a full-time job."

"That was probably the most helpful explanation I've received to date." Those words gave me great insight into this new life of mine. Funny thing was, I couldn't remember the last time the North Pole or any part of my old life came into my thoughts. It no longer mattered, what did now was my new family that I loved and adored and who loved me in return.

It wasn't long after that Grace came by to pick up Kaleb, and she too stayed for lunch. We discussed my vision for the baby's room, for which I really didn't have one and relied heavily on their input. I had no clue what Monty and his brothers had planned for it and being a big fan of surprises, I was good with that. Kaleb would be with us since Aiden was helping with our baby's room while we shopped and that was fine by me. Kaleb and I bonded, and I loved being around the little guy.

"Sandy, would you like to hear the baby's heartbeat?"

Her face lit up. Grace popped off the couch and ran to her bag.

"Let me grab my stethoscope. Why don't you lie back on the couch, Twinkle."

I assumed the position and waited for Grace to find our cookie's heartbeat.

"It's stronger and louder every day, Twinkle. Here you go, Momma." Grace handed Sandy the ear plug part of the stethoscope and held the metal part in place on my belly. Sandy's excitement was contagious and had the three of us grinning wide.

"Oh Twinkle, it's so beautiful. Thank you for letting me hear this." Sandy's eyes teared up, as did mine and Grace's. Family was important. Family was everything.

"What are you two hens doing with my mate?" Monty said as he walked inside.

"Listening to your baby's heartbeat. Get over here, son, and listen for yourself." Sandy's no-nonsense tone had nothing but love behind it.

"Mighty happy to oblige." Monty took the earplugs from Sandy and a second later he smiled wide. "That right there is the most beautiful sound I've ever heard, and I can't get enough of it. Is there a way to record this?"

Grace got that thinky face look. "That's a great question. I've heard stories where after childbirth, the heartbeat has been recorded and the recording placed inside of a stuffed bear. Then whenever they wanted to hear it, they pressed the button, and it played. But I'm not sure how to do that in utero. Let me get back to you on that."

"Yay!" My excitement could not be contained. The thought of having our baby's heartbeat available to play whenever we wanted was just, I don't know, it gave me all these happy bubbles.

"Alright, Momma," Grace said as she put the stethoscope away. "Let's get Kaleb and head home. I think we can pass the torch to Monty."

We said our goodbyes, and off they went down the mountain. Monty showered and we settled in on the couch until that inevitable time of day hit and I took off down the hallway.

"So much for cuddling and movie time." I complained as Monty scooped me up and carried me to bed, as he did every night as of late. "I love our baby with all my heart, but this has really cut into our alone time." When was the last time we even made love? Sex for me had become one of those things where you as soon as you opened it, you were addicted and couldn't get enough. Now I felt so yucky all the time that perk fell to the wayside.

"Sorry, my love, but we can watch it from bed. The movie, I mean."

"Your mom brought prepared meals with her. I froze all but one figuring I wouldn't be able to cook...Again." This was ridiculous. How did omegas do this time and again?

"Twinkle, you're fixated on things you shouldn't be. While I appreciate your desire to take care of me, I am capable of feeding myself. You worry about you and our little bee."

"Cookie."

"Cookie? I think you've been hanging around Kaleb too much."

"No, I call her our little cookie."

"Her?"

I shrugged. "I don't know for sure, but I just have a feeling it's a girl."

"A girl, huh?" Monty got this far away look and smiled. "A sweet princess. Wouldn't it be fun to make her room look like a castle?"

"I'm no genius so maybe hold that thought until we receive confirmation, Papa."

"Papa. I like it." Now that we'd both said it, though I'd only voiced it to myself, it was perfect.

Daddy and Papa it was.

Chapter Twelve
Monty

"Monty?"

"Yes, my whiney princess?"

"If our cookie is your princess wouldn't that make me your Queen?" He huffed. That belly of his stuck out so far he could no longer see his shoes.

I bowed. "Yes, my Queen, what is thy bidding?"

"Did you hear that, Princess Cookie? Papa made me a queen!"

Grace told Twinkle and I that it was good to talk to the baby once Twinkle passed the five-month mark and that they could actually hear us then. Didn't have to tell him twice, Twinkle did it every chance he got, and it was freaking adorable.

"Don't be like your Daddy, you want to be on the nice list." Twinkle's eyes widened and he froze. "Twinkle, are you all right? What's wrong?" I grabbed my phone and prepared to call Grace.

"Feel this." Twinkle grabbed my hand and placed it on his belly.

"Whoa, is that?" It happened again. "Is that Papa's princess kicking?"

"It is!" Twinkle spun around and nearly tipped over, but I caught him. "Thank you, Monty bear. Guess spinning is out of the question for a couple months."

"Yes, it is, my love. Does the baby kick a lot?"

"It just started a couple days ago. At first I thought it was gas, but nothing came out and then it happened again. I called Grace and she laughed and told me it was the baby kicking."

I tried to hug Twinkle, but it proved challenging given his belly, so I settled for a kiss. "That was one of the most wonderful things I've ever felt." Shit, even to my ears that didn't sound right.

"What if we keep calling the baby princess and it's actually a prince? Will that be bad?"

"My love, I think gender is irrelevant, but our love is what matters and clearly our cookie is happy." At least, I hoped kicking equated to happiness.

Twinkle tried to stand on his tip toes as he had many times before to kiss my cheek though this time the poor guy couldn't manage. "You're gonna have to lean down so I can kiss you, Monty bear." Kiss complete, he waddled down the hall and into the baby's room.

He was so enamored with the room after my brothers and I completed it, that I'd often find him fast asleep in the rocking chair beside the crib. Our baby's dreams would be filled with happy thoughts as it fell asleep each night in its *cow jumped over the moon* themed room.

Grace had come up with the idea and my brothers and I hand painted the scenes and clouds on the walls. I found clear LED twinkle lights we hung from the ceiling that lit the room like shiny stars in the night sky. The pale, baby blue walls were the perfect backdrop that made the room warm and inviting.

My sister Jolie found this adorable white, cloud-shaped rug we put in the center of the floor. The LeClaire kids' crib was in need of a facelift and took a bit more time to complete than I'd planned but turned out great. The white clouds and moon I painted on the footboard popped against the dark wood of the crib.

Jolie found the perfect crib sheet and blanket set online that she ordered for me. My father made the dresser and painted it white as well. With the crib and the rocker in dark wood, the white served to brighten the room.

Momma went a bit overboard, which Twinkle would see at his shower this weekend. Currently the drawers and changing table were empty but that would be short lived. My family was a bit overzealous given it was my first child.

A quick glance at my watch warned me it was about time for Twinkle to run for the bathroom. I got the crackers and soda ready and set it up on his nightstand. Warm wash cloths awaited him on the vanity.

I waited.

And waited.

Thirty minutes later when he didn't tear across the hall I feared the worst, that he'd gotten sick in the baby's room. Twinkle would never forgive himself for that.

I burst into the room, expecting to find a mess and instead startled my poor pregnant mate who had been asleep in the rocking chair.

"Twinkle, I'm so sorry, I didn't mean to scare you." I kneeled in front of him, his fist still tightly clenched in his shirt as he caught his breath.

"Why did you do that?" His breath was heavy and ragged and not in a good way.

"I was afraid you got sick in here. It's that time."

He started at me, blinked a few times, then it sunk in. "I-I, I don't feel sick."

Dare I hope for the best? Was the morning-afternoon sickness behind us?

"Isn't this room dreamy?" The way Twinkle swooned over the finished product. It was like he was seeing for the first time again though he'd been in here a million times already.

"It is and so are you. Feel like braving supper tonight?" Grace wasn't worried about his weight loss, but I was, and I knew from this point on the baby required more sustenance.

"I could go for a hamburger. Ohhh and fries. Too bad we don't have chocolate shakes. And pickles. Lots and lots of pickles."

My turn for the blink-blink.

"Actually, I believe we do." Should I have pointed out that burgers were meat? He'd never forgive me if I didn't. "Um, you do realize that hamburgers are meat? Cow meat, specifically."

"Nooo!" Twinkle burst into tears. "No cows!" He pointed to the one on the wall jumping over the moon.

"Cows are friends, not food. Is there, is there," he stuttered and wiped his eyes. "Veggie burgers?"

"Okay, okay," I'd do anything to stop this. "Let me see what I can do."

> Me: Momma, Twinkle wants a burger but a veggie burger. How do I get that? Need to stop the tears.

> Momma: Ah, hormones. Be gentle with him and FYI, there's a box of them in your freezer.

> Me: You're a genius.

> Momma: Tell me something I don't know. Now go feed my future son in law and grand baby.

"Baby, it's okay. Momma already hooked us up."

He burst into tears again. "I have to pee."

"Okay," I gave him a hug. "You um, you take care of that, and I'll take care of dinner."

"'Kay." He wobbled off toward the bathroom but at least this time it wasn't to vomit.

I was happy to report, dinner stayed down and my pregnant mate soundly slept beside me.

Thank fuck that was behind us. Now, onto uncontrollable hormones.

"Are you nervous?" Momma whispered as Twinkle mingled with the rest of the family that were here for the baby shower.

"Yeah, a bit. Remind me again why I chose today to do this?"

"You've got this, Monty. That man is head over heels for you."

"Before or after presents?" Timing was everything today.

"During."

Like that made it any easier...

Kody and his wife Grizelda and their three kids, Kaleb, Kora, and Kolton were here. The kids were outside playing in the fenced area with Tina. Glad I'd had the foresight to set up a slip and slide and some outdoor toys for them.

Seth and his wife Emmy got here first. Emmy brought enough food to feed an army or in this case an army of hungry LeClaire's. I was glad my family had taken the reins on setting this shin dig up because I hadn't the first clue how or what to do.

Joe and Anna's two kids, Kadence and Kam, yes, my family seemed to have something going on with K names for some odd reason. Their boys were outside as well. Meanwhile Jolie and Tanner, who took after my parents and kicked out four tic-taks had just arrived. I had a hell of a time remembering their names and they were so close in age I'd had yet to find any characteristics to associate with them to pin the correct name to the child.

Grace and Aiden came with Momma and Dad, Twinkle was sitting with Kaleb on his lap. He was sad when he could no longer crawl around with Kaleb when he watched him, but he'd never be able to get up on his own if he had.

"Wow, that is one huge pile of presents." Tanner said as he walked up.

"Yeah, I don't even know what to say." We'd have fun later washing everything and putting it away. I knew Twinkle was looking forward to that part.

Grace took Kaleb from Twinkle as Momma walked up to him. "Thank you everyone for being here for this momentous occasion." She winked at me and my hand immediately shot to my pocket. "I know for many of us, we never thought Monty would find his mate. He'd likely have slept through their visit and missed then all together. Then along came Twinkle. So full of life and such a happy man. He is a welcome addition to this family." The crowd riled and whistles rang out. "Fill your plates and grab a seat and Twinkle will start opening his gifts. While he eats too, of course. Can't have the pregnant one not eat."

"I'll fix his plate."

"Love you Monty bear."

"Love you too, sweetheart."

"Awe," rang out but I couldn't care less. I wore love well, no matter what my siblings thought.

There was a special bag with a special empty tiny box in it buried in the pile of presents. Only me and Momma knew which one it was but when she handed it to him that was my cue.

"Oh my gosh, Monty, look at the tiny flannels. The baby will look just like Papa."

"Hopefully it's better looking," Joe called out and the brothers laughed and I fought the urge to shoot them the bird.

Tiny hangers, reuseable diapers, biodegradable wipes, lotions, shampoos and a baby monitor. I swear we'd have enough to last until our child graduated. Hell, at this point I needed to build a storage shed to keep it all in. Twinkle and I purchased the pumping kit on our own, he felt it was too personal to have someone else buy it for us.

"Sandy," Twinkle teared up. "Did you make this?" He held up the blanket he'd just opened.

"Each panel is a piece of Monty's baby clothes, and the backside is his baby blanket." She'd worked on that for weeks and it turned out great.

Twinkle was a ball of tears. Momma winked at me, and I knew I was up. I watched as she handed Twinkle the bag. He took the little box out and opened it. "It's empty." When he turned toward me, I'd dropped to one knee in front of him. I heard a faint, "Oh my Goddess," come from one of my sisters but my focus was on Twinkle.

"Twinkle. You came into my life, a whirlwind of sugar filled energy and turned it upside down. In the best of ways. You loved me even when I didn't love myself. You've dealt with my grumpy butt and showed me what it's like to fall in love. Twinkle, the love of my life, the father of my child. Will you do me the honor of adding the word husband to that list?"

The room was silent. My heart madly raced as Twinkle's tears spilled over. "Yes. Goddess, yes Monty. I love you so much."

I slid the ring on his swollen finger and shot out a silent thanks to Momma for talking me out of sizing it before the baby came. Damn woman was insanely smart, though I'd never tell her that.

Cheers rang out as we kissed.

"Little snowflakes all the way around it. Oh Monty, I can't believe how perfect it is."

"It's a one of a kind, designed and created just for you. The sapphires match your beautiful eyes that I'll never grow tired of staring into."

Chapter Thirteen
Twinkle

"Monty, do you think there's enough lights on the tree?" I stood back, assessing his hard work. He wouldn't let me near the ladder, couldn't say I blamed him. As it was I could barely walk a straight line let alone balance above the ground.

"Sweetheart, if we put anymore lights on it we'll alert the NASA space station currently orbiting the earth."

"Pfft," I huffed and grabbed another cookie. "The stockings over the fireplace are perfect. I love the one for our cookie." We had the most Christmassy house on the mountain. Well, I thought we did. Monty said this was the first time he'd not only put up a tree but decorated inside and out. When he picked up the packages in town of all my orders he'd thought I lost my mind.

Maybe just a bit...

"They do. Are you warm enough? Can I get you anything?"

The closer I got to delivering the more of a nervous Monty he became. The impending winter storm didn't help any with that. We'd bought an additional freezer that we put in the mud room and stocked full of meals just in case we got snowed in.

"Yes, I'm warm enough." I plopped down on the couch and instantly regretted it. "Can you help me up. I want to make sure the baby's room is clean."

He stared blankly at me.

"What?"

"Okay..." he dragged the word out like I'd spoke a foreign language.

"The tree is perfect." Monty insisted on cutting the tree from our own land which was beyond romantic, and he promised to replace it by planting a new one in the spring.

When he finally got me up, it took a couple of tugs, I decided I wanted to dust instead and grabbed the cloth we used for that. Since Christmas was tomorrow, everything had to be perfect.

Monty typed away on his phone while I got to work. Christmas tunes played in the background, which was a bit of a heated discussion but in the end sass, snark, and tears won out and we'd had them on ever since.

"Can you put the rest of the presents I wrapped under the tree please? They're on the counter."

"Of course, here," he handed me a cup of cocoa with a candy cane sticking out of it.

He got me, he really got me. And yes, I still watched far too many romance movies.

"Thank you, my love."

Tonight, the whole family would be over to exchange gifts, barring the storm, though they all believed we had another day or two before it would hit. I wasn't allowed on the snowmobiles, given my condition, so they decided our house was best for the LeClaire holiday festivities. Fine by me, I was most comfortable here.

"It looks like the gifts are all lined up, waiting to be loaded onto Santa's sleigh." There were so many presents they were under the tree, beside the tree and along the adjacent wall.

"Tons of nieces and nephews to spoil and many for our cookie monster."

The first time Monty said that I burst into tears, afraid he thought our baby was a literal monster. He calmed me down and turned Sesame Street on and showed me who it was. I felt foolish but ended up enjoying the show and even ordered a stuffed cookie monster for ours.

"Merry Christmas!" One by one the family piled in. I was perched in the recliner Monty purchased when I could no longer get myself out of precarious furnishings. This chair had an additional feature that pushed the unit forward and helped you stand. Best invention ever and it came with a remote control.

"Twinkle, stay put," Sandy said, "we'll come to you."

Everyone fixed their plates and Sandy brought me mine. "I made this special for you and I promise it's animal free."

"Thanks, Sandy."

"Twinkle, what did I tell you?"

It tugged at my heart to say it as I'd longed for one of my own for so long. "Thanks, Momma."

She kissed the top of my head. "You are very welcome, sweet boy. Now feed my grandbaby."

My only contribution to this meal was a ton of sugar cookies. They weren't as immaculately decorated as normal, Monty had to help me, and his hand wasn't as steady.

More like his attention to detail was sorely lacking but we had fun making them. At least, I did.

The kids were getting restless, as was I though mine wasn't for presents. Levi played Santa, fake hat and all and handed out the presents.

"Are you okay, Twinkle?" Monty whispered to me.

"Just cramping up. I might have to pee for the thousandth time today."

"How long have you had cramps?"

"Off and on all day."

"Wait, what?" His voice was loud enough to startle those standing near. "Why didn't you tell me?"

"Seemed inconsequential. I've been restless and uncomfortable for the last few days and figured I'd eaten something the baby didn't like." My cravings were bordering on outlandish as of late. Peanut butter and jelly with a side of dill pickle slices and for some reason I wanted olives on everything though Monty said no way when I tried to put them on my pancakes this morning.

Monty flagged Grace down who came right over. "Cramping?"

"Yes."

"Any blood?"

"Not that I've noticed but I haven't done, you know, anything that needs to be wiped." Hadn't pooped for two days now and it felt like I was about to in my pants. "Feels like I have to now though."

"Monty, it's time."

I swear the entire room went silent, kids included.

"I'll line the bed with towels." Sandy headed toward our room, but Monty just stood there.

"Monty, snap out of it. Your mate needs you." Grace's voice rose and he finally came around. "Get Twinkle up and walk him back to the room. Now."

Monty came and helped me up while the others started cleaning up the wrapping paper and the kitchen.

"Ow! Ow! Ow!" I stopped halfway down the hall when the strongest cramp I'd had yet hit me. As soon as it subsided another followed. At the slowest pace known to man, I made my way down the hall, stopping with each contraction until I finally made it to our room.

"Close the door, Monty, and undress Twinkle."

Momma, Grace, Monty and I were the only ones in the room.

"Twinkle, do you want me to leave?" Momma asked. We hadn't decided whether or not to have her in the room but right now, I needed her grounding force.

"No, I need you."

"Anything for you, sweetheart."

Momma helped Grace get the bed ready while Monty stripped me down. I was in far too much pain to care who saw my bits and baubles.

"Twinkle and I discussed it, and he opted for a standard, non-water delivery." Grace let Momma know. "Twinkle, let's get you situated so I can see how far you're dilated."

Just as she reached for my underside another contraction hit. "Ahhhhh!" I clenched my jaw and rode out the pain.

"He's nearly there, at eight centimeters and I can feel the baby's head."

"Twinkle, we only have a moment for you to decide if you want me to run the numbing cream around your opening. Yes or no?" Grace asked. She'd already gloved up and had the container in hand.

"Yes please, as long as it won't hurt the baby."

"It won't." It warmed as she applied it, then the sensation dulled.

Monty sat beside me and held one of my hands, Momma on the other. The love in this room was overwhelming. My life was so full and on the brink of becoming fuller with the birth of our little cookie.

"Twinkle, it's time. When I tell you to push, you need to push as hard as you can."

"My back is killing me."

"Monty, move him forward and lay a pillow down then put him back in place. That will relieve some of the pressure."

The discomfort at being moved in this state was not fun, but I refused to say that and risk upsetting Monty, though I nearly screamed.

"All right Twinkle, it's time. Now Push!"

"Ahhhhhh!" I screamed as I bore down and pushed with all my might.

"Nearly there. The head is crowning. Push!"

"Ahhhhh!"

Back and forth we went between relax and push, and I thought I might pass out. What kept me from giving up was that tiny body Monty and I made that we were dying to meet.

"Shoulders are next. Push, Twinkle!"

Too exhausted to scream, I bore down and pushed with what energy I had left. "No more," I muttered. My body was tired, my brain ached and I'm not even gonna mention what my bottom half felt like, the numbing cream long since wore off.

"Good, because she's here."

"She?" We had a daughter.

"Yes." Grace laid her on the portable scale she had. "All eight pounds of a beautiful, healthy, baby girl. Monty, cut her cord." She handled Monty the scissors and he snipped. Grace wrapped her in a blanket and handed her to Monty.

"Hello, Luna. Welcome to the family."

"Luna?" I whispered.

"Yes, Luna. She's shines as brightly as the moon." He handed her to me. "Luna, meet your Daddy."

"Hello my beautiful Luna. Welcome to the light." There wasn't a dry eye in the room. Monty, me, Momma and Grace's eyes spilled over with happy tears.

"I'll get the warm water so we can get her cleaned up and she can meet the clan. You did great, Twinkle. Congrats Daddy and Papa." Grace left the three of us with our amazing daughter.

"You were right all along, Twinkle. We were having a girl."

"Ah telepathy between carrier and carry-e.," Momma said. Not sure if that was a real word but I'd let it slide. "I knew with each of the kids what their sex was but never said it aloud for fear of jinxing it. Oftentimes I wondered if they didn't communicate that detail with us while we kept them warm and incubated."

Grace washed our sweet girl up and one by one the family funneled in to meet her. Blessings and well wishes were shared for our Christmas miracle born just after midnight.

After the others left, Grace did one final check, and made sure Luna latched onto my nipple and fed.

"It's important to have that connection with your baby. Your milk is the best thing for her right now. If she were to reject it we'd have to try a formula. If you have any issues with her or with healing, call me immediately."

"Thank you Grace, for everything. I love you," Monty hugged her.

"Love you too big brother and love you as well, brother Twinkle." With a final hug she, Aiden, and Kaleb left.

"Our little Christmas miracle," Monty said.

"Yes, she is," a familiar voice replied.

"Santa twenty-seven!" I whispered, shocked to see him here.

"Congratulations, Twinkle and Monty. She's beautiful as is her namesake."

"Thank you," we both replied as one.

"Monty, nice to formally meet you."

Monty nodded. "Santa, how do you know my name?"

"Santa knows everyone's name, it's his job."

"That's right. Twinkle, you've changed your life around and become the elf I knew you could always be."

"I'm not an elf, not any longer. I'm a LeClaire." Monty proudly puffed up at my words.

"That being said, I'll grant you one last wish. What one thing would you like to have from your old life before we part ways for good?"

I glanced down at my sweet princess Luna and up at Monty, my wonderful fiancé and Papa to our girl. Her eyes, blue like mine, and her hair as dark as his. She had so much already.

"Thank you for the offer, Santa, but everything I need is right here."

"Not even to wish for your beloved elf ears back?"

"No. Ears don't make the man. The choices the man makes in life does and while there was a time my choices were less than stellar, that time is no more. I'm exactly where I'm meant to be."

"That you are, Twinkle." Santa turned to Monty. "Monty, I believe you've got this under control."

"*We* have this under control. Twinkle and I are a team."

"That you do. Twinkle, I'm very proud of you. You've not only fulfilled the stipulations set upon you in order to remain human, but you've fallen in love and have made a beautiful family with your mate."

I glanced down at the beautiful life that Monty and I had created.

"Yes, we have, and I couldn't be happier."

"*We* couldn't be happier," Monty corrected. The love radiating from my soon to be husband filled me with a warmth that no Yuletide fire ever could.

"Merry Christmas, LeClaire's."

"Merry Christmas, Santa," Monty and I replied.

Santa disappeared just as quickly as he'd come.

"And a very Merry Christmas it is," I said to our sweet girl.

"The best. You've made me the happiest man in the world, Twinkle. I promise to love and protect you and our Luna for as long as I live."

There wasn't a doubt in my mind of that.

Merry Christmas to all!

Love,
The LeClaires

Grab the rest of the books in the Santa's Naughty Elf Mates series

About TL Travis

TL Travis is an award-winning published author of LGBTQIA+ contemporary and paranormal romance, and erotic musings that have earned "Best-Selling Author" flags in the US as well as Internationally.

In her free time, TL enjoys catching up with her family, attending concerts, wine tasting, and traveling.

TL is surrounded by her extensive 4-legged rescue pets and growing family. She will continue saving furry friends in need for as long as she lives. Tl would like to remind you to "Adopt, not shop." Saving that lost soul may be just what you need.

Other books by TL Travis

The Social Sinners Series:

Boxset:

https://books2read.com/SSWorldTour

Behind the Lights, 1

MM Coming of Age Rockstar Romance

In the Shadows, 2

MM Rockstar Hurt/Comfort Romance

A Heart Divided, 3

MMM Rockstar Romance

Beyond the Curtain, 4

MM BDSM Hurt/Comfort PTSD Rockstar Romance
After the Final Curtain, 5
MM BDSM Rockstar Romance
Bonus Story
Diamond& Easton's Vegas Elopement
MM Rockstar Romance

Maiden Voyage Series:
Boxset
Ryder's Guardian, 1
MM Rockstar Bodyguard Romance
Derek's Destiny, 2
MM Rockstar Teacher Romance
Jaxson's Nemesis, 3
MM Enemies to lovers Rockstar Romance
Shadow's Light, 4
MM Rockstar Hurt/Comfort Second Chance Romance
Bonus Story
Claiming the Guardian
MM Rockstar Bodyguard Romance

Embrace The Fear (ETF) Series:
Rhone'sRebel, 1
MM Hurt/Comfort Rockstar Romance
David's Disaster, 2

MM Daddy-boy Hurt/Comfort Rockstar Romance
Seltzer's Taylor, 3
MM Rockstar Romance
His Final Chase, 4
MM Rockstar Daddy-Little Romance
10/25/2024

Chaotic Abyss Series
Strike a Chord, 1
MM Rockstar Second Chance Romance

Daddies and their Littles
When Daddy Hurts
MM Daddy-Little Hurt/Comfort Romance
A Little Christmas: Jacob
MM Daddy-Little Hurt/Comfort Holiday Romance
A Little Christmas: Orion's Secret
MM Daddy-Little Hurt/Comfort Holiday Romance
A Little Christmas 3: Ralphie
Coming 12/13/2024
MM Daddy-Little Hurt/Comfort Holiday Romance
Two Daddies for Henry
MMM Daddy Hurt/Comfort Found Family Romance
A Little's Valentine's Party: Featuring Jacob & Orion
Daddies and Littles Series

Pet Play

Pick Us, Daddy

Pride Pet Play 2023 Series

https://books2read.com/PPP2023

Ahoy Daddy!

Pride Cruise 2024 Series

MM Daddy Romance

Daddies:

Pints 'n Pool

Foggy Basin Series

MM Daddy Small Town Romance

Pints 'n Pool Holiday

A Foggy Basin Short Story

Coming 12/7/2024

https://books2read.com/PintsHoliday

A Daddy for Christmas: Brighton

MM Daddy Holiday Romance

A Daddy for Christmas 2: Jobe

Coming 12/13/2024

MM Daddy Holiday Romance

Mpreg/Shifter novels:

Naughty Elf: Twinkle: M/M Mpreg Shifter Christmas Romance

https://books2read.com/TlTwinkle

Standalone novels:

Heat

MM Small Town Coming of Age Bear Bottom Romance

See Me

MM Hurt/Comfort Enemies to Lovers Body Positive/Disfigurement Romance

Greyson Fox Saga (each can be read as a standalone):

Greyson Fox

MM Erotic May/December Age-Gap First Time Coming of Age Romance

Forgive Me Father

MM Coming of Age Hurt/Comfort Rent-a-boy Romance

Stand-alone novelette's/novella's:

Summer Boy

MM Small Town First-Time Coming of Age Demisexual Romance

Girl Crush

MF (1 scene)/ FF Sapphic Romance

What Works For Us
FF Over 40 Erotic Novelette
Rules of the Game
MM Erotic Workplace Romance
Coffee, Tea or Me?
MM Contemporary Romance
Snowed In With You
MM Contemporary Second Chance Holiday Romance

<u>**Paranormal Romance:**</u>
The Sebastian Chronicles
Historical Paranormal Erotic Romance
(Includes all 5 stories listed below)
Sebastian, The Beginning
MF Historical Paranormal Erotica
My Servant, My Lover
MF/MM Historical Paranormal Erotica
Wealthy Ménage
MF/MM/MFM/Ménage Historical Paranormal Erotica
Prohibition Inhibitions
MF/MM/MMF/MFM/BDSM Historical Paranormal Erotica
The Tryst - Chronicle Finale
MM Paranormal Erotic Romance
Pity the Living, Not the Dead

MM Paranormal First Time Dark Romance

MF Titles are published under Raven Kitts